Targeted Risk

R.I.S.C. Series Book 7
Anna Blakely

Dedication

This book is for those of you who've been here from the beginning. I'm not sure how you first found me, but I'll be forever grateful that you did. Not only did you take a chance on me when I was a newbie, you're still here. Still coming back for more. For that, my heart and my characters thank you!

Another person I need to give a HUGE shoutout to is my editor, Tracy Roelle. I'm beginning to think she just might be as crazy as me, because no matter what life decides to throw at me while trying to finish a story, and no matter what's going on with *her* life, she always manages to make time for me. Big hugs, Tracy! Love you bunches!

Last, but not least, I'm also dedicating this book to the real Lydia, whose soft fur and quirky personality make me smile on a daily basis. Yes, this soft, furry feline is real, and she's even more of a spaz than I was able to describe in the book. But we love her!

XOXO ~
Anna

About the Book

HE'LL TRUDGE THROUGH THE DEPTHS OF HELL JUST TO KEEP HER SAFE.

Returning to the dangerous world of deep cover is the last thing Mike Bradshaw—former Delta Force operator and newest member of R.I.S.C.'s Alpha Team—wants to do. But just when he thinks he's finished with covert life for good, Mike discovers the woman he left behind—the woman he still loves—is in danger. Determined to protect her, he must once again become the man Juliet believes him to be. A man who doesn't really exist.

Trust doesn't come easy for Juliet. Having a father in the Russian mob could do that to a girl. Then she meets Mike—the mysterious, tattooed man sent to protect her. Before long, lines are crossed and the love Juliet never thought existed is found...until the life she'd built for herself is suddenly ripped from her hands, and Mike disappears without a trace.

When Mike unexpectedly waltzes back into Juliet's life, neither can deny the same magnetic pull that first drew them together. Soon, however, their newly formed trust is put to the ultimate test when secrets are revealed, and hearts are broken. Even worse, someone still wants Juliet dead.

Determined to save the woman he loves, Mike will stop at nothing to get the target off Juliet's back. After all, he's the one who put it there.

Prologue

Twenty-two months ago...

"We got him."

"What?" Mike Bradshaw sat straight up. The three words his government handler had just spoken sent his heart racing.

"You heard me," CIA Special Agent Benjamin Lopez answered. "It's over, Bradshaw. You're going home."

Holy shit.

Swinging his legs over the edge of the bed—*her* bed—Mike glanced down the hallway toward the kitchen. Turning his voice to a hushed whisper, he asked Lopez, "Mikhail finally talked?"

"Something like that. Listen, are you with the sister?"

Mike looked toward the kitchen, again. He could hear Juliet moving around in there but didn't see her. "Yeah. We're at her place. But wait. The world thinks Mike Bradshaw died ten years ago." An unfortunate necessity to do the job for which he'd been assigned. "How am I going to explain—"

"We'll go over the details later. Just get out of there. Now."

Alarm bells rang inside his head at the man's curt tone. "Why? What's going on?"

Before Lopez could answer, Juliet hollered from the other room. "Hey, Jay? Do you want bacon or sausage with your eggs?"

Jay Reynolds was his undercover name. One he'd grown to fucking hate.

Shit. "Uh...surprise me," Mike answered with a casual tone. That tone changed when he spoke into the phone again, demanding his handler give him an answer. "Talk fast, Lopez. Why the sudden urgency for me to leave?"

"I'll explain everything when you're clear. For now, you need to listen to me and do what I say."

Before Mike could argue further, he heard a knock coming from the front door. A man's muffled voice immediately followed.

"Miss Volkov? This is the FBI. We need you to open the door."

What the fuck?

A mass of dread grew into a fiery pit inside Mike's stomach. "The Feds just showed up, Ben." He hopped out of bed. Using his shoulder to hold the phone to his ear, he quickly threw on the pair of boxers and jeans still crumpled on the wooden floor. "What the hell is going on?"

"Goddamn it," Lopez cursed loudly. "I told them to stand down until I gave the order."

"What order?" Mike started for the hallway at the same time Juliet exited the kitchen.

Wide-eyed, she looked to him for an answer he couldn't give. "It's the FBI. What should I do?"

"I gotta go." Mike started to end the call but stopped when he heard Lopez holler at him to wait.

"Keep your cover, Bradshaw," the other man commanded. "We can't risk fucking this up because you're thinking with your dick."

"Fuck you."

There was another knock. "I can hear you, Miss Volkov. Please don't make this any harder than it needs to be."

"Jay?" Juliet urged him to guide her next move.

The first thought that came to Mike's mind...how much he longed to hear his *real* name fall off those ruby red lips. *If wishes were horses, beggars would ride.*

"It's okay, Jules," he assured her. "I'm sure they're just following up from the last time they were here."

Clearly not buying his explanation, she hugged herself and shook her head. "It sounds like they're here to do more than just talk."

Swinging her gaze to the door then back to him, her long black hair fell over her shoulders and halfway down the snug white t-shirt she had on. Glancing at the phone in his hand, she asked, "Is that my Mikhail? Ask him if I should answer the door."

No, baby. It's not your brother.

"Just go with it, Mike," Lopez instructed him through the phone. "Keep your cover while she's within earshot. Stay calm and do as they say, and you'll be headed back to Dallas by this time tomorrow. Who knows, you may even make it back in time for your sister's wedding."

Fuck.

"Jay?" Juliet looked to him again, her sapphire eyes filling with fear.

"Everything's going to be fine." Mike had no more uttered the lie when someone burst through the front door, its wooden frame splintering from the force.

Startled, Juliet screamed as a group of men stormed their way into her apartment. "What are you doing?" she asked. "This is my home. You can't just barge in here like this."

"We need you to come with us, Miss Volkov." A man donning a navy-blue FBI jacket approached her. "We have a court order to take you in for questioning."

Mike recognized him as FBI Special Agent Thomas Fuller. He'd been in on some of the meetings Mike had attended while on this assignment. The guy was a total dickhead with a major ego trip.

"Like hell you do." Ending the call, Mike shoved his phone into his pocket, covering the distance between him and Juliet in three, long strides.

"Questioning?" She swung her gaze back to his and then to Fuller. "For what? And I go by Farrow, not Volkov. Farrow is my mother's maiden name."

"He knows that, Jules." Resting his hand on her lower back, Mike glared at the man in front of them. "He's just being an asshole."

Ignoring him, the asshole in question directed his next comment to Juliet. "I'm Special Agent Fuller, Miss Farrow. We've been led to believe you hold pertinent information that will help with the case against your father."

"My *father?*" Her laugh held no humor. "I haven't spoken to Alex in years. I certainly don't know anything about whatever it is you think you have against him this time."

The arrogant agent shrugged. "Our intel says otherwise."

"Yeah?" Mike stared the other man down. "And what intel would that be?"

Because it sure as shit wasn't the intel he'd given them. His latest job had been to turn Juliet's brother, Mikhail, against their father. If Mikhail agreed to testify against Alexandar Volkov, they'd finally be able to put the piece of shit behind bars for good.

Getting close to Juliet had been Mike's backup plan. One that began to fall apart the second he'd first looked into those spellbinding blue eyes of hers.

According to what Lopez had just relayed over the phone, they already had Volkov. So why had these guys just busted Jules' door in?

"That's none of your concern, Mr. Br...uh...*Reynolds.*" He eyed Mike up and down. "Nice ink, by the way."

Seriously? The asshole damn near gave away his cover and he was complimenting his tattoos? The entire, shady scenario caused the pit in Mike's stomach to grow at an alarming rate.

Ignoring Lopez's earlier demand that he play nice, Mike said, "I want to see the court order."

"Sure." Fuller handed him the folded papers. "We'll head to the car while you're reading that over." Grabbing Juliet by her upper arm, he began pulling her toward the door.

Mike lost his shit, then, shoving the agent with both hands. At the same time, Juliet managed to pull herself free from the dickhead's grasp.

Fuller turned his narrowed gaze on him. The prick snapped his fingers, sending two of his men into action. They went for Mike, then.

Taking a swing at the closest one, he laid Tweedle Dee out with one punch. Unfortunately, Tweedle Dum had anticipated the move. Taking advantage of Mike's split focus, the guy cranked Mike's hand behind his back, simultaneously kicking the back of his knee, sending him straight to the floor.

"No!" Juliet yelled. "Leave him alone! Jay has nothing to do with this!"

Ah, baby. I wish that were true.

He wished a lot of things were true.

With fire in her eyes, the brave woman actually jumped onto the agent's back, trying to get Tweedle Dum off of Mike. At the same time, the other agent still standing nearby grabbed hold of Juliet's shoulders.

Wrong move, asshole.

"Get your fucking hands off her!" Mike growled as he fought to get free. A useless endeavor given that Tweedle Dee had risen to his feet and joined in the effort to keep Mike subdued on the floor.

The two men shoved him the rest of the way down.

"Like Agent Fuller told your girl..." Tweedle Dum spoke calmly. "Don't make this any harder than it has to be."

"Fuck you."

Using more force than necessary, the man still holding onto Juliet pulled her roughly toward the door.

"Jay!" she called out for him, the terror and confusion in her voice ripping his heart to shreds.

With one side of his face now smashed against the cool, hardwood floor, Mike lifted his eyes to meet hers. God, he hated the fear he found there.

"It's okay, baby," he told her again. "Just go with them. I'll be okay."

"No. I'm not leaving you!" She kept fighting against the man's strong hold.

"Not your choice." Fuller picked up the court order that had fallen to the floor during Mike's struggle. To the man holding onto Juliet, he tipped his chin and said, "Get her out of here."

"Wait! You can't do this. Just...wait!" Juliet's pleas went unanswered as she was dragged out of the doorway and away from Mike's sight.

Knowing she couldn't hear him—and no longer caring, even if she could—Mike shot Fuller a seething glare. "You son of a bitch. I'll have your fucking badge for this."

"You can try." The man's lips curled into an arrogant smirk. "But I'm just following orders, Bradshaw. Just like you were when you started playing house with our target's daughter. Right?"

Turning to leave, Fuller stopped when one of the guys holding Mike down asked, "What about him?"

The dickhead purposely pressed his knee into the middle of Mike's back, causing him to grunt. *Goddamn, that hurts.*

Glancing down at him, Fuller instructed his agents, "Cuff him. Wait until we leave, and then bring him in."

"She doesn't know anything," Mike spoke through a set of clinched teeth as one of the fuckers on top of him cinched their cuffs around his wrists.

"Is that information coming from Michael Bradshaw, CIA Para-military Operations Officer?" Fuller grinned. "Or Jay Reynolds, the guy she thinks has been sleeping with her sweet ass?"

"You son of a—" Mike tried fighting the two men again, but it was no use.

"Keep him here until we're clear. I'll meet you back at headquarters." Fuller started to leave again, but then stopped for a second time. "And make sure you bring him in through the front and not the back. Just like you would any other suspect."

"You sure?" one of the two men asked.

Fuller nodded. "As much as I'd love to see the look on Farrow's face when she learns the truth about who he really is, letting that particular cat out of the bag too early could screw the pooch on this one."

Without another word, the asshole finally left Juliet's apartment. As ordered, the men holding him down waited until he'd driven off before picking him up and planting him on his feet.

"Come on, man." The bigger of the two nudged him forward. "We're all on the same side here, right?"

The only side Mike was on was Juliet's, but damn it...he wouldn't be any good to her if he continued acting like a full-blown alpha protector.

"Yeah, asshole." He glanced over his shoulder. "We're on the same side. So why don't you take these fucking things off me?"

Tweedle Dum shook his head. "Can't. You heard the boss. Not until we're inside the station."

"You know how this works, Bradshaw." Tweedle Dee spoke as he took the lead. "Cuffs come off once we have you in a secured room, away from the Volkov chick."

"It's *Farrow*, you prick." They approached the black SUV. "And how many times do I have to tell you assholes. She's not associated with her father."

Tweedle Dee glanced back at him as he opened the back door. "You sure about that? 'Cause Fuller said—"

"I don't give a rat's ass what that douchebag said," Mike cut him off. "I've been working this case for a long fucking time, and I'm telling you, she's clean."

"Yeah? Then why did a judge sign off on an order to bring her in?" Tweedle Dum asked.

"Fuck if I know." But he would damn sure find out.

On their insistence, Mike climbed into the backseat.

"Watch your head," one of the men warned.

Better watch your fucking back.

The second the door was shut, Mike closed his eyes and drew in a deep breath. Damn it, these guys *were* on his side. At least they were supposed to be.

After ten years of playing the game, he was finding it harder and harder to determine the good guys from the bad. For now, he had no choice but to do as Lopez had instructed and go along with this bullshit.

An hour later, he was still waiting in an interrogation room inside Las Vegas' FBI headquarters. Like a common criminal.

That's what you're supposed to be, remember?

The sound of metal clanging together filled the small room as Mike rested his elbows on the table in front of him. Becoming antsier by the minute, his right leg began to bounce as he waited for someone to come in with an update on Jules.

When he was about two seconds away from going postal on all their asses, the door to the room opened and Benjamin Lopez walked in carrying a t-shirt and a manila folder. Of medium height and build, the middle-aged man with his dark hair and pressed suit looked more like a lawyer than a CIA handler.

"Where the hell have you been?" Mike shot out of his chair.

"Relax." Lopez walked over to him. Pulling a set of keys from his jacket pocket, he tucked the folder under one arm and motioned for Mike's hands. "Let's get those off of you."

"Don't tell me to fucking relax. I've been sitting in here for over an hour." He lifted his bound wrists toward the other man. "Where's Jules?"

Releasing the cuffs, Lopez pocketed both them and the keys before giving Mike the shirt. "Juliet Farrow has been taken into federal custody."

"Why?" Mike put his arms through the sleeves and pulled the shirt over his head. "I told you a thousand times, she's not part of her father's business."

"Maybe not, but she knows several players who are. Both brothers, included."

"Bullshit."

Lopez handed him the folder. "This is a list of names associated with Alexandar Volkov's illegal dealings. The Feds have reason to believe your girlfriend possesses intel on at least one of the names on that list. Possibly more."

"Jules isn't my girlfriend." Mike flipped opened the folder and began scanning the list of names. Having worked the Volkov case for nearly a year, now, he recognized most of them immediately.

"Of course, she isn't. She's Jay Reynolds' girlfriend, and you and I both know he doesn't actually exist. But you know who does?" Lopez, the fucker, paused for dramatic effect. "Special Agent Michael Bradshaw. You happen to see him around? Tall guy, shaggy beard, tats that probably drive all the girls wild..."

Asshole.

"You should get your eyes checked, then, because I've been here the whole time."

"Have you? Because lately, I feel like I've been dealing with an angry, overprotective boyfriend rather than an undercover agent in charge of bringing down the leader of the worst Russian mob syndicate to ever hit the U.S."

"I've done my job, Ben." Mike shut the folder and slapped it against the man's chest. "I've gotten you closer to Volkov than any other agent to date."

"Closer, yes. But the man's not behind bars just yet."

"You said Mikhail agreed to talk."

"He did."

"Then what do you need Jules for?"

"Corroboration."

"For what? Jesus, man. I've told you, she—"

"Knows more than she's led you to believe."

"Bullshit. Her mother left Volkov when Jules was still a teenager. They moved to a small town just outside Kansas City. She told me all about it."

"Yeah? Did *Jules* also happen to mention the secret trips she took to Vegas without her mother's knowledge?"

"What the hell are you talking about?"

"According to her brother, after Juliet graduated high school, she started visiting Alexandar. She knew her mother would never allow it, so she lied. Claimed to go away for a school function or a girls' weekend away. The story was always different, but there was at least one trip to Vegas every summer. And, according to Mikhail, each of those trips were spent with her father. Not with a bunch of sorority sisters, like Juliet told her mother."

"Mikhail's probably just saying that shit so he's not alone in the Let's Bring Daddy Down plan." Chickenshit bastard.

"Possible, but unlikely."

"What makes you so sure?"

"Because when Mikhail told us about his sister coming to visit, he did so as a bargaining chip."

A what? "You're not making any sense, Ben. So she lied to her mom about going to see her dad. Even if that's true, it was a long damn time ago. And it's only natural for a daughter to want to spend time with her father."

Especially if that daughter didn't understand the kind of man her father truly was.

"Mikhail agreed to turn state's evidence against his father and older brother, but only if we could guarantee his sister's safety."

"Why does he think Jules wouldn't be safe?"

"Same reason you were able to convince him to keep you close to her in the first place. To protect her from possible backlash by her father or Ivan. Or both."

Mike ran a hand over his beard. Three months ago, he'd been with Mikhail, still trying to turn him, when his sister had stopped by unexpectedly.

At the time, Mikhail was still wavering on whether or not to testify against their father. Mike, along with the other agents on the joint task force trying to bring Volkov down, had worked too damn long and too damn hard to risk losing this one. For him, Juliet was another way in. So, after she left Mikhail's place that day, Mike had gotten him to believe his sister needed protection.

It hadn't taken much coaxing to get the other man to agree, and once they came up with a plausible story about one of their father's enemies making threats, Mikhail had convinced Juliet to let Mike hang out with her. Just as a bodyguard of sorts.

The plan was a win-win for Mike and had made the higher-ups extremely happy. Mikhail was even more convinced than ever that Mike was on his side, and he also had an in that allowed him to determine whether or not Juliet was more than the sweet, innocent sister Mikhail claimed her to be.

It took less than a day for Mike to realize she was nothing like her father. Or her brothers.

"I pulled that shit about Alexandar and Ivan going after Jules out of my ass, and you know it," Mike reminded Lopez. "I only said that to get close to her. See if she knew anything...which, as I've been pretty clear about, she doesn't."

"Maybe. Maybe not." Lopez shrugged. "She lived in the same house as the man until she was fifteen. She could've learned a hell of a lot in that time. Add to that, Juliet's secret visits to her dad when she got older, all taking place during the time in which his business took off, by the way, all bring me back to this." Lopez held up the folder.

Fuck. "You think she may have seen or overheard something during her visits to her father. Something involving one of the men on that list?" Mike shook his head. "If Jules had witnessed her father or brother participating in anything nefarious, she would've said something."

"Jesus Christ, Bradshaw." The guy looked at him as if he'd lost his damn mind. "Stop thinking with your dick for two seconds. The woman's father is a big dog with the Russian mob, for Christ's sake. You think she's just gonna pick up the phone and spill her guts to a random nine-one-one operator?"

"No, asshole. But she would've told *me*."

"Why? Because you're banging her? Give me a fucking break." Lopez tossed the folder onto the table. "You said she hasn't seen or spoken to her father in years. Why do you think that is?"

Bastard.

"I'm not saying she's not aware of what Volkov does for a living, Ben. What I'm saying is, she wanted no part of that life. That's why she cut herself off from him."

Lopez refused to back down. "Question is, did she cut herself off because she finally understood what her father was and what he did for a living, or because she witnessed something horrific and couldn't stand the thought of being around him anymore after that?"

"She said they grew apart. And I believe her."

"Because, and I return to my earlier assessment, you're thinking with the little head in your pants instead of the one on your neck."

"I've stuck this *neck* out for you and your agency for ten fucking years, Ben. I've given my life to the CIA, and to you. You've trusted me on every op, and I've come through for you every single time, so why the hell can't you trust me, now?"

"Because you've made this one personal." The agent got up in his face. "I'm not stupid, Mike. You love this woman. I can see it in your eyes every goddamn time you say her name."

He didn't deny it. "She. Doesn't. Know. Anything."

Taking a deep breath and a step back, Lopez ran his fingers through his hair before resting both of his hands on his hips. "Do you remember what you said when you called to tell me about your little bodyguard assignment idea?" When Mike didn't respond, the agent proceeded. "I do. You told me she might be a way in. That there was a good chance she knew all about her father's dealings. That she may even be able to give up some names. Your words, Mike. Remember?"

Yeah, he fucking remembered. "So?"

"So it was a good call. One the prosecutors want to pursue in a more formal capacity."

Sonofabitch. "You do realize now that you've brought both Juliet and her brother in, it's only a matter of time before her father finds out. What do you think Volkov will do when that happens, Ben?"

"I imagine he's going to assume they're both giving him up. Hence the protection part I tried explaining earlier. If you're right about Juliet and she knows nothing about her father's illegal business, then great. We can use Mikhail's testimony, along with information you've gathered, to put Volkov away for good. After that, your girlfriend will be free and clear to go on as if nothing ever happened."

"That's great, except, even if Jules doesn't testify under oath, her father is still going to be suspicious. He'll always wonder if she turned on him, too. When guys like Alexandar Volkov get suspicious..." *People die.*

"Goddamn it!" Mike locked his hands behind his head and blew out a breath. "How long until she leaves?"

"She's already gone, brother. Witness Protection took her twenty minutes before I got here. She's been assigned a new name and a new city to live in. A member of the federal prosecutor's team will question her on the plane. Determine if there's anything there to work with. Either way, Juliet will have twenty-four-hour protection until after her father's trial."

"And when will that be?"

"Judge hasn't set a date yet, but he's expected to within the next few days. In the meantime..." Lopez pulled a white envelope from his jacket's inner pocket and held it out.

"What's this?"

The other man smiled. "Your walking papers. Of course, you'll have to stay tonight and give your official statement. Plus, you'll most likely be called to testify, although that will be behind closed doors to protect your alias, just in case. But yeah...it's over, kid."

Mike's pulse spiked as he ripped open the envelope and pulled the single-page letter free. Scanning it quickly, he realized the man was telling the truth. After ten years of trudging through the shitholes of hell hidden deep in this country's dark crevices, the CIA had declared him to be a civilian.

The letter went on to explain the backstory behind Mike's "death" to the outside world, but none of it resonated with him because all he could think of was...

I'm free.

"See? I told you you'd be home for your sister's wedding. Which reminds me." Lopez handed him a second envelope. "First-class ticket to Dallas-Ft. Worth. Your flight leaves at eleven a.m. tomorrow."

I'm going home.

Ben slapped a hand on Mike's shoulder. "You did good, Mike. Real good. I know it's been a long time coming. Much longer than any of us could have anticipated." He held out that same hand. "But on behalf of the CIA, the President, and the entire country, thank you for your service."

Mike didn't know what to say, so he shook the man's hand in silence. His long-term, deep cover gig was officially over, which meant he finally had his life back. A life he'd given up ten years prior in order to make the world a safer place.

A life that doesn't include Jules.

He knew he should be happy. Ecstatic, even. But in that moment, a part of him wished he could stay Jay Reynolds forever.

****

Chapter 1

Present day...

"I'm out." Mike tossed his cards face-down onto the table.

"Again?" Jake McQueen, Mike's boss and brother-in-law frowned. "That's what, four in a row you've folded?"

"Give or take."

Derek, his new team's technical analyst, collected the discarded pile and set it to the side. "Oh, I'm happy to take, brother." The former SEAL grinned. "In fact, I'm perfectly fine takin' your money all night long."

"Pretty sure you've been taking *all* our money tonight, dickhead," Coop muttered unhappily as he threw down his own hand.

Derek shrugged. "Not my fault y'all suck at Three Card."

Staying in the game, Trevor Matthews—Alpha Team's medic and second in command—tossed a few more chips into the growing pile in the center of the table. "Night's still young, West. I wouldn't go running that big mouth of yours too soon."

"Matthews is right," Grant Hill—the biggest and from what Mike had observed so far, the most stoic member of the team—glanced down at his hand before finally deciding to stick it out, as well. "And you'd better not be doing that counting cards bullshit you tried pulling last time."

"I'd listen to the big guy, if I were you," Coop recommended. "Dude's a former SEAL and an explosives expert. You screw Grant over, he'll probably turn that little car of yours into a fireworks display."

"I was a SEAL, too, asshole." Derek shot Coop a look as he dealt out the requested cards. "And any of you fuckers touch my Challenger, I'll steal your identities and give them to some jagoff in some third-world country. I'm sure they could use the money."

"And on that note..." Jake smirked as he stood.

Grant glanced up at their boss. "You out for good?"

"Nah." Jake shook his head. "Just getting another beer. Anyone else need one?"

"I could use one, Boss." Coop held up his near-empty bottle.

"Me, too." Derek grabbed his and chugged what was left of his.

Trevor swished his bottle around and nodded. "Make that three."

"I'll go with you." Mike stood. "Besides, I've lost enough money to West for one night."

Derek held out his hands and grinned. "Don't hate me 'cause you ain't me, brother. Hey!" He ducked when a couple of the guys threw pretzels at the smartass.

Mike chuckled as he walked into the kitchen. Grabbing the bottle opener, he began opening the beers as Jake handed them to him. The sound of light laughter pulled his attention away.

Across the room, the women were all gathered around Lillian Rose, Mike's six-month-old niece. Olivia—Mike's little sister and Jake's wife—was sitting on the rug in front of the large, stone fireplace. She was playing peek-a-boo with her young daughter, who was giggling up a storm every time her momma uncovered her eyes.

Mike's heart swelled at the sight.

"They're something else, aren't they?" Jake stood beside him.

"Yeah." Mike nodded with a smile. "They're something, all right."

Every time he looked at Olivia, Mike felt a mixture of guilt and gratefulness. Guilt for having let his little sister—and everyone he'd ever cared about—believe he was dead in order to go off and save the world. Grateful because, despite having done that, his sister had forgiven him, welcoming him back with open arms.

He also felt grateful as hell for the man standing next to him. If it hadn't been for Jake, they would've lost Olivia two years ago to the hands of a madman. And if that had happened, little Lillian Rose wouldn't be here, either.

The little girl giggled, causing the other women around her to follow suit, and a sudden flash of a different child entered his mind's eye. Another young girl with jet black hair and crystal blue eyes.

Just like Juliet's.

Somewhere along the way, intertwined with his memories and lifelong regrets, Mike's mind had created her. She wasn't real, but God, he wished she was.

"Knock that shit off, Bradshaw," Jake practically growled in his ear.

"What?"

"You know what. Jesus, man. You've been back almost two years. Forget about that shit, already. I know she has."

His heart thumped hard against his chest, and it took Mike a second to realize Jake was talking about his sister and the guilt he still felt for having left her. Of course, the guy wasn't talking about Juliet. He didn't even know she existed.

None of them did.

There'd been a few times since he'd been back when Mike had been tempted to tell his brother-in-law about her. Times when it was just the two of them shooting the shit over a cold beer and a warm fire. But just thinking her name was hard enough.

Saying it out loud? Forget it.

She had a different life, now. One she'd never be able to share with him, because she only knew him as Jay Reynolds. An alias he'd given up the day he'd walked away.

Not that he hadn't thought about looking her up. Just to check on her and make sure she was okay.

Mike glanced over at Derek who was giving the other guys shit while collecting his most recent winnings. If anyone could find her, it would be him. Of that, he had no doubt.

The guy was insanely smart, and when it came to computers and searching for data and intel, there was no one better for the job. Still, Mike hadn't asked D to find Juliet. What would be the point?

According to Ben Lopez, Mike's former handler, both her father and her older brother had been tried and convicted of sex trafficking and several other heinous crimes he'd committed during his reign with the Russian mob. All thanks to the testimony of Volkov's youngest son.

If Juliet was smart—which she was—she would've kept the false identity the Feds had given to her while in their protective custody and used it to reinvent herself completely.

That's what Mike would've done if he were her. Hell, he *had* reinvented himself...several times over. But now, even though he was back home, close to his sister and working alongside the friend he'd known since elementary school, part of him still felt...lost.

"Earth to Mike. Hey." Jake nudged his shoulder. "You okay?"

He blinked, snapping out of the self-torturous haze. "Huh? Yeah." Mike forced a smile. "Sorry."

With a knowing stare, Jake asked, "Old ghosts coming back to visit?"

Mike shrugged. "Sometimes they never leave, ya know?"

"Yeah." Jake glanced over at his wife. "I do, actually."

Mike looked over at Olivia and Lillian again. It still broke his heart to think of what his sister had been put through while he was still under cover and that he hadn't been here to save her from being kidnapped and tortured. Thankfully, Jake had been.

"I think I'm gonna head home," he told Jake somberly.

His friend looked at his watch. "Already?"

"It's been a long week."

Rather than laugh or make some sort of smartass comment, Jake stared back at him with an assessing gaze. "You sure you're okay?"

"Yes, Mom. I'm fine." Despite his sarcastic words, doubt began to seep in as he glanced over at the guys again. "Why? Has someone complained about my performance on the team or something?"

"What?" Jake swung his gaze to the table and back to Mike. "Hell no, they haven't said anything. Nothing bad, anyway. In fact, Mac told me the other day that it felt as if you'd been part of the team from the beginning."

The Mac Jake was referring to was McKenna Kelley, the only female member of Alpha Team. Like Coop, who was also her fiancé, Mac had been an Army Ranger prior to joining R.I.S.C. Also like Coop, the woman was one hell of a sniper.

"Speaking of Mac..." Mike decided to change the subject. "How come she never plays cards with us?"

"Because I work too damn hard for my money."

Speak of the devil.

Both men turned to see the woman in question approaching them. Standing all of five-five with long, blonde hair and big blue eyes, Mac looked nothing like the deadly operative Mike now knew her to be.

"One of those for me?" She eyed the bottles of beer on the counter.

"Sure." Mike handed her one, then went to the fridge to get a replacement. "And I only asked about you not playing cards because I noticed none of the women do." He glanced over to where two other wives were still hanging out and talking by the fire. "Didn't want you thinking y'all weren't welcome at the table with the guys."

"Oh, don't worry, brother." Jake took a swig from his bottle. "Mac knows we're an equal opportunity team, here. Don't ya, Mac?"

"Yep." The adorable government-licensed killer grabbed the bottle opener from Mike's hand. "These guys all know I could pick them off in their sleep from a hundred yards away if they ever pulled any of that male chauvinist bullshit with me or any of the other girls. But I prefer to spend my money on tangible things like shoes and handbags, rather than line the pockets of my oh-so-endearing teammates."

The sugary-sweet smile she gave them made Mike snicker. "Shoes and handbags?"

Mac grinned. "I keep forgetting that your new-ish. Jake? Maybe you should fill him in. I have to go get more Lilly cuddles before my poker-impaired fiancé over there loses his share of our monthly freebie allowance."

Jake nearly spit out his beer. "You put Coop on an allowance?"

"We *both* agreed to cut back on our frivolous spending. Weddings are expensive as hell."

"Not if we had it here!" Coop hollered across the room. Thanks to the open floor plan, the young sniper had obviously overheard the conversation.

It still floored Mike that the teams two snipers were engaged. Most teams like theirs would separate couples if they became romantically involved. Too much of a risk for personal issues at home affecting their performance and concentration on the job. But somehow, Coop and Mac made it work, so Jake allowed it.

"That's right." Jake nodded. "Liv loved the ceremony we had out back. And Grant and Bryn had theirs here, too. It's like a R.I.S.C. tradition, now."

"The Bravo Team guys have all done their own thing," Mac pointed out with a grin.

A little over a year ago, Jake decided to expand the business and hired on a second team of guys to help with the overload of ops being thrown their way. Mike hadn't spent much time around those guys, but from what he knew of them, they were as solid a team as the one he was now a part of.

"Okay, fine." Jake stood corrected. "It's an *Alpha* Team tradition, then. Either way, there's more than enough room, and more importantly, it would be free."

"He's right." Olivia walked into the kitchen area with Lilly propped up on her hip. "We'd love to host the ceremony. But only if that's what *you* want. It's your wedding, after all."

"Ahem, isn't it *our* wedding?" Coop butted into the conversation again before tossing down his cards with a scowl. "Damn it."

"Free location or not, there won't be a wedding at all if you lose every time you come here."

"Not true." Coop stood and headed their way. "One, I'm still within the limits of my budgeted spending, and two"—he snaked an arm around Mac's tiny waist and pulled her to him—"there ain't nothing gonna stop me from marrying you."

The room groaned in unison as their teammates shared a kiss.

Mike chuckled, but inwardly he was filled with an unfair resentment toward the young couple. "Think that's my cue to leave." He grinned. "But first, I'm going to go say goodbye to my adorable niece."

Taking the baby from his sister's arms, he relished in the little girl's soft, sweet warmth. His lips pressed against the smooth skin on her rosy cheeks, the smell of baby lotion filling his nostrils as he held her close to his chest.

"She loves you so much." Olivia beamed up at him. "So do I."

"What's not to love?" Mike downplayed his sister's sentimental comments, but then he locked his gaze with the beautiful bundle in his arms.

Lilly's round, brown eyes—ones that matched her mother's to a T—lit up. She squealed and flailed her chubby little arms about as she reached toward his face. Before she could dig her tiny but sharp nails into his chin, Mike gently turned her small wrist in order to kiss Lilly's palm.

"Uncle Mikey loves you, too, Bug."

Growing up, he'd called Olivia Junebug. First as a joke due to her aversion to the brown, crunchy creatures but then as a term of true endearment. When Lilly was born, he could instantly see she was the mini version of her mother, so he decided to give the baby the shortened version of the same nickname.

With another squeal, he kissed Lilly's forehead before handing her back over to her mother.

"I think this *bug* needs a bath before bedtime." Olivia smiled up at him. "Wanna do the honors, Uncle Mikey?"

"Actually, I think I'm gonna head out."

"Already?"

Jake laughed. "That's what I said. I think your brother may have lost his edge in his old age."

"Old age, my ass." Mike scowled playfully at his friend. "I could still whip you."

"Still?" Jake raised a dark brow. "Funny. I don't recall you having whipped me any other time."

"Hmm..." Mike pretended to act concerned. "Maybe my sister should be more concerned about your memory loss than my edge."

The group laughed as the two men continued bantering back and forth for a good minute before Mike finally called it a night.

"Come on." Jake slapped Mike on the back. "I'll walk you out."

Giving his sister one last hug, Mike said his goodbyes and followed his brother-in-law to the front door. Still giving a polite nod and a wave, he did his best to ignore the scene playing out at the table to his right.

Poker game momentarily forgotten, the other R.I.S.C. wives in attendance had left their spots by the fireplace to join their husbands, Trevor and Grant.

Lexi, Trevor's wife, was sitting on his lap and laughing while Brynnon, Grant's very pregnant wife, was smiling as her husband ran his big hand over her swollen belly.

The entire scene looked like something out of a Norman Rockwell postcard. One Mike wished he and Juliet could be painted into.

Enough, already! Christ, man. You're like a pathetic broken record.

The voice was right. He needed to move on. Needed to forget all about Juliet Farrow and their make-believe love story. What they had was long gone. *She* was long gone, and everything they'd shared had been based on nothing but lies.

Not all of it was a lie.

No, what Mike felt for the sweet interior decorator was the most real thing he'd ever felt in his life. And what sucked huge ass donkey balls was Mike was sure she was on the same page as him.

"Okay, spill it. What's going on with you?" Jake asked the second they stepped out onto his covered porch. "Is this all too much too soon?"

"What? No." He shook his head then blew out a breath. "Sorry."

"Quit fucking telling me you're sorry, and talk to me."

Shit. Rubbing a hand over his smooth jaw—something he still wasn't quite used to having—Mike walked over to the edge of the porch. Resting his hands on the railing, he looked out over the impressive piece of land his friend owned.

"You've really built something special here, Jake."

"Thanks. From what you've said, you have damn near all of your CIA paychecks stored away in the bank. You could have something like this, too."

"I'm not just talking about the house." He turned his head toward his friend. "I mean all of it. The house and the land are great. But you've also got Liv and Lillian to share it with. Hell, you've got the whole package, man."

"You could have that, too, if you'd...I don't know...maybe try going on a date sometime."

Mike couldn't help but smile. "I'm good but thanks."

"You're a shitty liar."

"A decade of successful undercover work says otherwise."

"Okay, fine. You're a shitty liar when you're trying to lie to *me*." Jake leaned a shoulder on the nearest porch pole and crossed his arms at his chest. "Seriously, Mike. Things are going great with the team and everything, but when we're not on an op, you seem...I don't know. Down or something. And I'm not the only one who's noticed. Liv's worried about you, too."

"My sister has always worried about me. Even more so since I've come back from the dead."

"Because she loves you."

"Yeah, I know." Mike looked up at the darkening sky. He hesitated a half a second longer, and then sighed. "Fine. You want to know the truth, here it is. I met someone."

"What?" Jake stood erect again. "That's great! When? Who is she?"

Mike held up a hand. "Ease up on the twenty-questions, dude. It's not like that. At least...not anymore, it's not."

"What do you mean?

"I mean, I met her when I was under."

"Okay..." Jake let his voice trail. After a slight pause, his brows rose, and a look of understanding crossed his face. "Oh."

"Yeah. *Oh.*"

"So, she has no idea who you really are," Jake surmised.

"She couldn't." Mike shrugged. "I was still 'dead', remember?"

"Okay, but what about after?"

Another shrug. "I left Vegas. So did she."

"And you never told her? Not even then?"

Mike shook his head. "I couldn't."

"Why not?"

"It's...complicated."

And you're full of shit.

The look Jake was giving him now said he thought the same thing. "I'm a pretty smart guy, Mike. I'm sure I can keep up."

Damn. He should've known Jake wouldn't let this one go.

Mike swallowed past his innate desire to keep things close to the vest. An occupational hazard a lot of undercover operatives have to learn to overcome once their covert time is complete.

They had to re-train their brains to allow for trust again. Not an easy task after a decade of not being able to trust anyone.

Every day since coming back home, Mike had to remind himself he wasn't alone. That Jake and the others were his friends. His new team. His family.

No time like the present.

"Fine. Do you remember the day Olivia found me with you in the barn?"

Jake snorted. "You mean the day my wife discovered the brother she thought she buried ten years before was alive...and I knew and didn't tell her?" He gave him a sarcastic stare.

"Guess it would be hard to forget a day like that, huh?" Mike shoved his hands into his pockets. "We talked that day about my last case I was working. The one involving—"

"Alexandar Volkov," Jake finished for him. "I remember. You were trying to turn one of his sons."

"Mikhail." He nodded. "Yeah. It worked, too. Mikhail's testimony put both his father and his older brother away for life."

"That's good, but what does any of this have to do with whatever shit you've got going on up in there?" Jake pointed toward Mike's head.

This is Jake. It's not like he's going to judge you. Just tell him, already.

"Volkov has a daughter."

Okay, so that was more of a blurt than he'd intended.

Jake closed his eyes and hung his head. "Ah, hell, Mike. Please tell me you weren't dumb enough to get involved with her."

"Told you it was complicated."

"Trigonometry is complicated. Fucking a Russian mob boss's daughter while you're trying to put the guy away is...shit." He ran a hand through his hair. "I don't even know. Suicidal maybe?"

"I didn't mean for it to happen, okay?" Mike jumped to his own defense. "When I found out he had another kid, I thought maybe I could use her, too. Just in case my angle with Mikhail didn't pan out."

"Sounds like you used her, all right."

Pushing off the railing, Mike faced his friend directly. "Fuck you. It wasn't like that."

"No? What was it like, then? Because you just said—"

"I know what I said, and I know what my intentions were with Juliet." He drew in a deep breath and forced himself to calm his shit. "Look. It was no secret the Feds were closing in on Alexandar. I convinced Mikhail his sister could be a target simply because she was Volkov's daughter. He contacted her. The guy kept my cover and talked her into letting me hang around to protect her."

"And he had no idea he was setting her up to be investigated, too?"

Mike shook his head. "No. My plan was to get close enough to her to find out if she knew anything about her father's business. Just in case Mikhail decided to turn tail and run or some shit. That's it. But then I met her, and...I don't know. The more I got to know her, the more we just sort of clicked. You know?"

"Yeah." Jake glanced toward his living room window. "I know."

Following his gaze, Mike saw what his friend was staring at. Both men had a clear view of the girls all standing around talking and laughing, but he knew Jake's eyes were focused solely on Olivia and their daughter.

"Then you also understand what it's like to care for someone so badly, you'll do whatever you can to protect them. Even if it means protecting them from yourself."

Jake brought his gaze back to Mikes. "Damn. It's like that?"

"It was. Yeah."

Exhaling slowly, the other man rubbed a hand over his scruffy jaw. "Okay, but all that shit's behind you, now."

"So?"

"So...you could go to her. Tell her the truth about everything without risking your job or letting some piece of shit skin trader go loose."

"Right. That would be a great conversation to have. I can see it, now. 'Hey, honey. I'm back. Oh, and by the way, my name's not really

Jay Reynolds. It's Mike Bradshaw. And I'm not really a friend of your brother's. I'm a former undercover CIA officer who used him and tried to use you to put your father and your other brother behind bars for the rest of their lives. What's for dinner?'"

"Okay, smart ass. Obviously, you'd approach it a little more delicately than that."

"You're not listening. I can't approach it at all."

"Why not?"

"She'd never forgive me."

"I thought the same thing about your sister, remember? And look at how that turned out."

"That's different."

"How?"

"You lied to Olivia to protect her. I lied to Jules because I was using her."

"At first, maybe. But I'm sure there was some truth to what you said about her father's business possibly making her a target."

"I could justify my lies all damn day, Jake. Doesn't change the fact that they were lies."

"Did you lie to her about how you felt?"

"No. I never...we never said..."

"You never told her you loved her?"

Mike sighed. "No. Because I knew there was no point. Just like there's no point in having this conversation."

"There is if you still love her."

"Love isn't the issue." Mike glanced out over the front yard again. "Hell, I don't even know where she lives, now. Last time I saw her, the Feds were dragging her out of her house. My CIA handler told me she was going into protective custody until they put her dad away."

"They use her, too?"

"Didn't have to. Mikhail testified. But they were worried someone would come after her. Use her to intimidate her brother into backing down."

"You've never looked her up? Never tried to find out where she went?"

Mike shoved his hands into his pockets again. "No point. Trust was everything to Juliet. She'd never forgive me."

"Don't you think she should be the one to get to decide that?" When he didn't answer, Jake said, "You know. I happen to know a guy who's really good at finding people who don't necessarily want to be found."

He's talking about Derek.

Pulling his keys from his pocket, Mike gave his friend's shoulder a squeeze as he walked past. "Thanks, Jake. But I'm good."

He was halfway down steps before Jake hollered behind him, "Like I said, man. You're a terrible liar."

Two hours later, while Mike lay in bed staring up at the ceiling, he'd begun to reconsider. Even if D did find Jules, that didn't mean he had to do anything about it. After two years of being apart, she was probably married. Maybe had a baby on the way or some shit.

The thought was like a steel-covered toe to the nuts.

But...if she *was* with someone else—as crushing as the idea was—then maybe, just maybe, he could move the fuck on.

The longer he laid there, the more tempting the idea became. Finally, after spending the night tossing and turning, Mike threw off the covers and grabbed his phone from the nightstand.

Several rings later, a very groggy Derek answered the call. "Someone had better be dyin.'"

"It's me." Mike drew in a deep breath and let it out slowly. "I need your help."

****

Chapter 2

Juliet Farrow held the two swatches of material up toward the light. "I can't decide between the inky blue or the vermillion red. What do you think?"

Lydia's only response was to roll onto her back and stretch.

"Thanks a lot." Juliet smiled as she bent over to scratch her cat's belly. "You're such a big help."

In response, the gray and white feline purred loudly with each stroke.

"Fine. I'll choose the color for the curtains later. You hungry?" The cat let out a tiny meow. "Me, too. Come on."

Relaxing like a wet noodle, Lydia allowed Juliet to pick her up and carry her into the kitchen. As they went, Juliet let her eyes wander around the townhouse she'd been renting for a little over a year.

With its contemporary style and private rooftop veranda, the renovated space was nice. But even after all this time, it still didn't feel like home.

Has anyplace ever felt like that to you?

When she was a young girl, maybe. But once she started getting older and was able to recognize when her parents were fighting or upset, her childhood home had felt more like a prison.

After she and her mother left, they'd rented a small apartment near Kansas City. A far cry from the million-dollar estate her father had built before she was born.

There was one time in her life—what felt like a lifetime ago—when Juliet had felt at home. But it wasn't the house that had made her feel that way. It was the man she'd begun sharing it with.

Jay had made her feel at home. He'd made her feel...*whole.*

"Nope." Juliet scratched Lydia behind her ears. "I'm not going there."

With her chin jutted out and her shoulders straight, she went to the cabinet nearest Lydia's dish and pulled out the bag of cat food. Once her food and water had been replenished, Juliet went in search of her own dinner.

Opening the refrigerator, she stared unimpressively at the foam container on the middle shelf. She thought of the frozen pizza in her freezer. "Which sounds better, Lydia? Leftover takeout or—"

Something creaked above her head, cutting through Juliet's words. Frozen, she held her breath and waited.

Though the townhouse had been completely renovated prior to her moving in, the bones of the place were still original, as were the hardwood floors. She'd learned early on which places creaked when stepped upon, and one of those spots was upstairs, in her bedroom.

Right above where she was standing, now.

"Did you hear that?" Juliet looked down at Lydia. The cat had stopped eating and her tiny ears had perked up. "Yeah. You heard it, too, didn't you?"

Her heartrate picked up its pace. The neighborhood was a quiet one on the outskirts of the city. Virtually no crime and very little traffic. Both major selling points when Juliet had first decided to relocate to Houston.

Still, low crime didn't mean *no* crime. As a single woman living alone, she couldn't take any chances. Especially one with a family as screwed up as hers.

If she'd learned anything from her vile father, it had been to trust her instincts...and no one else. She'd forgotten that rule only once, and the price of that lesson had been her heart.

Closing the stainless-steel door, Juliet slowly stepped away from the refrigerator. She picked up Lydia, as much for comfort as to protect her sweet cat and went for a small drawer nestled in the room's large island.

Doing her best to move silently, she pulled the drawer open and reached for the Kel-Tech PF-9 pistol she kept hidden there for protection. Another lesson she'd learned from her mob boss father...always be prepared.

And prepared, she was.

Along with the nine-millimeter gun gripped tightly in her hand, there were three additional pistols, a shotgun, and several knives hidden around her place. And she knew how to use each and every one.

Sliding the drawer closed, Juliet waited and listened. At first, there was nothing, which made her think maybe she'd imagined the eerie sound. But when she heard the creak a second time, she knew she hadn't.

With her heartbeat rushing through her ears, she slowly made her way out of the kitchen and to the winding staircase. Most women would probably take their cat and run, dialing nine-one-one as they fled to safety.

Juliet wasn't most women.

In her socked feet, she was able to climb the steps without making a sound. She moved quickly, hoping to reach the top of the stairs before whoever had been stupid enough to break in came out of her bedroom. Thankfully, she did.

Steadily holding the gun in front of her with one hand, Lydia lay curled in the other, nestling her head against Juliet's neck. Keeping her breathing steady and her footfalls silent, Juliet stopped to the side of her bedroom door and waited.

After several of the longest seconds of her life, a shadow appeared on the floor in front of the doorway. Her pulse spiked, and it became harder to breathe. If she'd had any doubts before, there were none present now. Someone else was in her home, and they most definitely had not been invited.

Halting her shallow breaths, Juliet swallowed back her fear and began to count down in her head. *Three...two...*

Dressed all in black—including his stocking cap and leather gloves—the masked man exited her room. During the seconds that followed, several things happened all at once.

Juliet yelled at him to freeze. The man started to reach for her. Lydia flew out of her arms, leaping straight toward the intruder's face.

Growling, the man ripped the cat from his mask and tossed her roughly to the side. Lydia landed on her feet then took off down the stairs in a dead sprint. At the same time, Juliet secured her weapon in her fist and took a step forward.

"Make another move and I will pull this trigger."

"Go ahead." Dark eyes stared back into hers. "There are more like me just waiting in the wind."

What?

Juliet's heart pounded against her ribs. "Who sent you?"

"You know who."

"Pretend I'm not that clever."

The man released a low chuckle. "Payback's a bitch, little Volkov. And so are you."

Before she could react, the man's hand shot out lightning fast. Grabbing her gun, she managed to get off one shot before he ripped it from her grasp.

Splinters flew from where the bullet hit the bannister's thick railing. A loud ringing filled Juliet's ears, but she ignored it and kept fighting.

Lunging forward, she kneed the jerk square in the balls then wrapped her fingers around the meaty hand still holding her gun. Remembering what she'd learned, Juliet used her own body's weight to throw the man off balance. They fell against the bannister, her body twisting together with his in an effort to regain control of the gun.

The gun that just fell through the railings and down the stairs.

Shit!

Assuming the guy brought his own weapon, Juliet wasted no time pushing herself off of him and running for her bedroom. Slamming the door behind her, she locked it as quickly as her trembling fingers would allow and ran for the French doors leading out onto her private rooftop veranda.

On her way, she stopped and grabbed the Glock she kept in her nightstand. Since it didn't have a safety, she kept that one there so she wouldn't have to waste even the half-second it would take to disengage before shooting.

Because those were the things one thought about after having grown up with a father who was a leader in organized crime.

Her mother, may she rest in peace, buried her head in the sand. For the first several years of her life, Juliet had, too. At first, it was because she didn't know any better. Then it was because she didn't want to know.

Later, during one of her secret visits with her father in Vegas, Juliet had no choice but to see the truth. Kind of hard not to when you witness the brutal abduction of a young, naïve stripper with your father standing idly by giving the orders. She'd never forget the smile the bastard had on his face when it was over.

Her bedroom door shook as the intruder slammed his body against it. Juliet yanked open one of the twin French doors and ran out onto the roof to hide. A total horror film chick move, but at this point, her options were limited.

The gun in her bedroom was the closest weapon from where she'd been. The veranda had a small alcove where she could conceal herself while she tried to regroup.

While she prepared to take a human life.

The sound of wood splintering let her know he'd made it into her room. The thumping of his heavy footsteps told her he was coming for her.

Juliet's chest physically hurt as her heart did its best to pound itself to freedom. She closed her eyes and drew in a deep breath, knowing her next actions would change her life forever.

"Dumb bitch." The man laughed. "Where the fuck you think you're gonna go?"

It's not where I'm going, asshole. You're the one about to leave...for good.

With her eyes wide open, Juliet slid her finger to the trigger and waited.

"I know you're back there, Little Volkov. Figured your daddy would've taught you better than to run onto a fucking roof to hide."

So she hadn't heard him wrong earlier. He'd used her given name. Her father's name.

"My daddy taught me a lot of things, asshole," Juliet hollered back. "Like how to shoot."

Before she could talk herself out of it, she jumped out from behind the narrow wall, aimed the gun, and pulled the trigger.

The man's entire body jerked. With help from the moonlight, Juliet could see his eyes widening with surprise through the oval slits in the woven mask.

"You...bitch." He dropped to his knees and clutched his chest. "Fuckin' shot...me."

"And I'll do it again if you don't stay down." Her words came out surprisingly steady, despite feeling as if she would fall apart at the seams.

It seemed the warning was unnecessary, for less than ten seconds later, the man had collapsed onto his back. Eyes closed. Chest not moving.

Ohmygod!

Juliet's breathing increased, but just before she could go into a full panic mode, she reminded herself of what needed to be done.

Call the police. Tell them you shot an intruder.

With her gun pointed at the dead man's head, she stepped in a wide berth around his body, turning so she could walk backward into her bedroom. Keeping an eye on the unmoving form, she made her way over to her nightstand and picked up the landline phone.

Dialing nine-one-one, Juliet forced herself to speak as she relayed to the operator the horrific events that had just taken place inside her home. Once the operator learned of the intruder's fate, she instructed her to stay inside and wait for authorities to arrive.

Most women would probably run outside, getting as far away from the corpse as possible. But again, Juliet wasn't most women.

Another lesson from Daddy...never make assumptions. Especially in a high-risk situation.

After ending the call, Juliet hung up the phone and went back outside. Chest still heaving, body fighting to regain control of itself, she watched the intruder warily as she approached him.

He was so still, almost like a statue. But he wasn't a statue...he was a human being. One who was currently bleeding all over her private oasis. A man who'd just died by her hands.

Oh, god.

A rush of burning bile hit the base of her throat, but Juliet swallowed it down. Sirens blared from somewhere in the distance, their screams getting louder and louder the closer they became.

She stared down at the masked face. A sudden need to know who he was and why he'd come after her was overwhelming.

Juliet knew she shouldn't touch him. That removing the mask could potentially be considered tampering with evidence. She didn't care.

I have to know.

Trembling legs carried her closer to the dead body. The gun in her hand quivered, despite her efforts to the contrary. Still, Juliet pushed herself on.

I have to know who he is. I have to know why he came after me.

Standing mere inches away, she bent down. Careful not to step in the growing pool of blood, she shifted the gun to her left hand and reached for the mask with her right.

Pinching the ends of the soft, black wool between her fingertips, she lifted the mask up and over the man's chin, revealing an unremarkable mouth and jaw. Still shaking, she started to raise the material over the man's nose when the unthinkable happened.

The man moved.

In one fluid motion, he grabbed hold of her wrist with one hand, yanking her fingers away from the mask, while at the same time, he pushed her body backward with his other.

Crying out from both shock and fear, Juliet fell onto the roof's hard surface with a painful thud. Blood dripped onto her chest as her very-much-alive attacker hovered over her, the barrel of her gun now pointing at *her* head.

"Please," she heard herself beg. "At least tell me why you're doing this."

"Why does anyone do anything?" The man grimaced in pain. "Money, sweetheart. And your father?" His exposed lips curled into an evil sneer. "He has a helluva lot to spare."

"M-my father? Are you saying...my *father* hired you to k-kill me?"

"You're surprised?" He chuckled then coughed. "What kind of daughter turns on her old man like that, anyway?"

Juliet shook her head with a frantic denial. "I didn't—"

"Shut up!" He pushed the gun closer to her head. "If you ask me, you've had this coming for a while."

"Good thing no one asked you."

Juliet heard his voice a split second before the retort of gunfire filled the night air.

****

Chapter 3

"Jules!"

Mike ran to where Juliet lay trapped beneath the man who'd damn near killed her. After calling Derek the night before to ask him to find Juliet for him, the guy had taken all of twenty minutes to track her down and call him back with an address...in Houston.

He couldn't believe it when Derek had called him with the news. For the past year and a half, Juliet had been right there, within his reach. All those nights he'd spent dreaming about her and wondering where she'd ended up, and she'd been three fucking hours away.

So he'd driven here, to the address Derek had given him. And then, like a coward, he'd sat in his car and waited.

For hours, he contemplated whether or not he should even walk up the townhome's steps. He went back and forth between what he should say and how he should say it. Played scenario after scenario of what *she'd* say and how she might react to seeing him again.

Before Mike knew it, the sky was turning dark, and he'd wasted the entire day sitting outside her house trying to get up the nerve to go talk to her. So he'd sucked it up and gotten out of his car. He'd barely made it across the street when he heard the first gunshot.

If he'd waited any longer...if he'd been ten *seconds* later...

"Get him...off of...me."

Her voice brought him back to the present.

"Juliet?"

When he got to her, she was struggling to push herself free. Filling his fists with the back of the asshole's shirt, Mike lifted the man's dead weight—literally— off of her and tossed him to the side.

With blood splattered and smeared all down her front, Juliet looked up at him with eyes as wide as saucers.

"Are you hurt?" he blurted as he held his hand out for her to take. "Did he hurt you?"

Rather than accept the help he was offering, Juliet slowly began to push herself to her feet. The wariness in her eyes seemed to seep down through the rest of her body.

"Baby, you're scaring me. Say something. Please."

"J-Jay?"

Shit. When he'd first gotten here, he had full intentions of telling her the truth. All of it. But seeing as how she'd been seconds away from being murdered in cold blood, Mike didn't think now was the time to drop that particular bomb.

"Yeah, baby. It's me."

One second, she was staring back at him as if he were a stranger. The next, she was flying into his arms.

"Oh, my God!" She squeezed him tightly. "I can't believe you're here!"

He couldn't believe he was, either.

"It's okay. I've got you, now. You're okay."

They stood like that for a full minute, holding onto one another as if neither ever wanted to let go. God, it felt good to have her in his arms again, even if it was under such fucked up circumstances.

"He was g-going to k-kill me." Her entire body shook against his.

"I know, baby. But he didn't."

Because I killed the motherfucker before he had the chance.

Still trembling, Juliet pulled away just enough to look up at him. "Wh-what are you...why are you—"

"Houston PD!" someone shouted from behind him. "Slowly step away from each other and put your hands in the air!"

Juliet's eyes shot up to his.

Mike let out a low curse. "Do as they say, honey."

"What?" She stepped out of his reach and around him in order to speak to the cop. "Wait, I'm the one who—"

"Get your hands in the air!"

Jumping at the man's fierce order, Juliet threw her hands high in the air. "M-my name is Juliet Farrow," she told the officer quickly. "This is my home. I called you because that man"—she pointed to the asshole bleeding all over her veranda—"broke in here and tried to kill me."

"You, in the leather jacket. Turn around slowly. And don't make any sudden moves."

Well, this is going to be fun.

Since getting shot wasn't on his list of things to do today, Mike followed the man's orders. Before him stood two uniformed officers, both pointing their guns in Mike and Juliet's direction.

"Officers, I understand why you drew your weapons, but I'm not the bad guy here. That would be him." Mike motioned to the dead guy lying a few feet away. "You know, the one wearing the ski mask and gloves."

"It's true." Juliet jumped to his defense. Pointing toward the intruder, she said, "H-he broke in here. *He's* the one who tried to kill me. I-I shot him in self-defense, but he was still alive. If Jay hadn't showed up when he did..."

"I take it you're Jay?" The officer in charge looked at him expectantly.

Damn it. "That's me."

"Okay, here's what we're going to do. Dorrell"—he spoke to the other officer—"pat them both down, and then take Miss..."

"Farrow," Mike and Juliet offered in unison.

"Right. Then take Miss Farrow into the other room and get her statement."

"Separate them." Officer Dorrell nodded. "Good idea."

A very, very good idea.

He didn't need Juliet overhearing that particular conversation. It was going to be hard enough to explain why the I.D. in his pocket said a different name than the one he'd just given the officers.

Officer Dorrell proceeded to pat them down, first Mike and then Juliet. When he was finished, he escorted a visibly shaken Juliet into her bedroom, shutting the door behind them for privacy.

"Okay, Mr. Reynolds. Let's see some I.D."

Here we go.

Keeping his voice low, Mike admitted, "My name isn't actually Jay Reynolds."

"Excuse me?"

As quickly and quietly as he could, Mike went through a short version of why he'd used that name. Smudging the lines between fact and fiction, he made it sound as if he were still working undercover for Juliet's protection. Then he went through the night's events starting with hearing the first gunshot.

After getting permission from the officer, he pulled out his real I.D., as well as the card Benjamin Lopez had given him in case he'd ever found himself in a sticky situation.

Pretty sure this qualifies and then some.

"The CIA?" The other man rose a skeptical brow.

"Look, Officer..." Mike glanced at the shiny name badge on the front of the man's uniform. "Lane. I know how all this sounds, but it's the truth. Just...call the number. And if that doesn't convince you, call this one." Mike pulled out another card. The one with the letters R.I.S.C. embossed on the front. "Ask for Jake McQueen."

Officer Lane's face oozed with doubt. "You know Jake McQueen?"

"You've heard of him?"

"Who hasn't?"

Thank fuck. "Good. Then that makes this even easier."

"Yeah?" Lane stared back at him. "Why is that?"

Mike smiled. "Because Jake McQueen is my brother-in-law. And my boss, although we grew up together, so it's still feels weird to call him that. Actually, I'm still not used to the whole brother-in-law title, either so—"

"Fine," Lane cut him off. "I'll make the call. But you stand right there and don't try anything funny."

Raising his hands palms-up, he assured the other man, "Wouldn't dream of it."

While he waited for Officer Lane to make the calls and verify his story—because yeah...even to him, that shit sounded crazy.

Mike glanced behind the other man and into Juliet's bedroom. Standing with her arms crossed in front of her, she was still talking with the other officer.

A nod here. A spoken word, there. And through it all, every so often, her gaze would shift in his direction. Damn, what he wouldn't give to know what she was thinking.

"Yes, sir." Officer Lane's voice snapped him back to attention. "I will. Thank you, Mr. McQueen. I appreciate it."

Mike watched him carefully as he ended his second call and pocketed his phone. "Well?"

"Well." The other man exhaled loudly. "Looks like you were telling the truth."

He raised a brow. "So what now?"

"Now I wait for my Captain to call to tell me how he wants me to proceed with this mess."

This made Mike smile. "Jake knows your boss?"

"It appears so, yes."

Of course, he does. Lucky for Mike, his brother-in-law seemed to know everyone these days.

Right on cue, Lane's phone began to ring. He was half-way through his conversation with whom Mike assumed was the guy's boss when Officer Dorrell started to come back outside. Thankfully, Lane gestured for him to wait, and he and Juliet went back into her bedroom.

Even from where he stood, Mike could see the confusion and worry crossing over her gorgeous face. With a wink and a grin, he did his best to assure her everything was going to be fine.

"Okay." Lane ended his third call of the evening. "Everything checks out."

"So, we're good?"

"We are." The man glanced down at the body lying behind Mike. "He's not."

"Listen, about the whole name thing..."

"Don't worry. Your cover will remain secure."

"Thanks, man." Mike held out his hand. "I appreciate it."

Returning the gesture, Officer Lane shot a quick glance over his shoulder then back to him. "She really Alexandar Volkov's daughter?"

Mike nodded. "Unfortunately for her, yeah. She is."

"Damn. Talk about a screwed-up family."

He let his grip tighten around the man's hand. "She's nothing like her father."

Lane pulled his hand free. With a shared look of understanding, he motioned for Officer Dorrell to rejoin them outside.

"Everything okay out here?" the younger officer asked.

"Hunky dory." Mike smirked. "Well, the dead guy probably wouldn't agree."

Juliet approached him with trepidation. Hugging herself again, she brought her eyes to his. "So what happens, now?"

"Now, we wait for the medical examiner and the forensics team to get here."

Hours later, both had come and gone. Juliet had been taken into the privacy of her bathroom and was picked over by a female forensic specialist. Once pictures had been taken and her clothes and other evidence from her person had been collected, she'd been given the go-ahead to shower.

For that, Mike was thankful, but there was still the issue of Juliet's entire home being marked off as a crime scene. That meant she could no longer stay there.

"Where am I supposed to go?" Juliet looked at the detective, who'd arrived shortly after they'd both given their initial statements.

Mike rested his hand on her lower back, the damp tips of her long, black hair brushing against his fingers. "You can stay with me."

"You live here, Mr...Reynolds?" Detective Morales gave him a knowing stare.

Okay, so he's been filled in on the situation and is playing along. Thank you, Jake.

"Dallas," Mike answered truthfully.

Surprise filled Juliet's blue eyes.

"Unfortunately, that won't work for us," Morales commented. When Mike opened his mouth to argue, the man said, "I understand it's a lot to ask, but we'll need you both to remain in the city of Houston until the medical examiner has completed the autopsy. As long everything else checks out there, you'll be free to leave. Until then, you'll both need to stay in town."

Juliet shook her head. "But—"

"It's okay." Mike smiled down at her. "We'll get a hotel room for the night. Surely, the medical examiner will be finished sometime tomorrow."

He could probably press the issue, given his connection with Jake and the CIA, but he needed these guys on their side.

The detective's expression was unreadable, but he gave Mike a slight nod. "I've already told Dr. Kidwell to push this case to the top of her list."

"Appreciate that."

Juliet's eyes bounced back and forth between his and the other man's. "Am I missing something?"

"Nah, baby. He just understands that you're the victim, here. This is obviously a clear-cut case of self-defense, and the Houston Police Department cares about its citizens. They want to ensure you're not inconvenienced any more than is absolutely necessary. Isn't that right, Detective?"

Putting his notepad and pen in his blazer's inner pocket, Morales cleared his throat. "That's correct. You've been through enough, Miss Farrow. We'll do everything we can to help you put this horrible event behind you as quickly as possible."

"Thank you." Juliet shook the man's hand.

"I'm assuming she's free to pack a bag and her necessities for the hotel?"

"Of course. My people have looked around, and it's obvious this was where the intruder entered Miss Farrow's residence."

The scratches on the French door's outer lock were a dead giveaway.

"Thanks again, Detective." Mike also shared a handshake with the guy.

"Mr. Reynolds."

Mike followed Juliet into her bedroom and helped her gather some things to get her through the night and the following day. She was acting a little strange, but given everything she'd been through, it wasn't a huge shock.

"Is this everything?" He zipped the small suitcase closed.

Biting her bottom lip, "Almost."

When she didn't make a move to grab anything else, Mike got a funny feeling in his gut. "What is it?"

Her gaze slid behind him to the activity still taking place on her veranda. "I have other guns," she whispered. "And knives."

"Okay..."

"They're hidden around the townhouse."

"Oh." Ignoring, for the moment, the fact that she'd felt the need to hide weapons around her home, Mike thought for a moment. "Well, the knives certainly aren't an issue. And this is Texas. Owning multiple guns isn't illegal." Most would say it was encouraged.

With an even more hushed tone, she gave him a hardened stare. "What if the guns weren't bought...legally?"

"If they weren't..." Mike swung his head around and looked outside. Morales was speaking to Officer Lane, and neither man was paying them any attention. He slid his gaze back to Juliet. "What the hell do you mean they weren't bought legally?"

"I mean, I bought them from a less than savory individual. You know, the kind that doesn't ask for I.D."

The smartass comment, along with the look she was giving him, made Mike want to turn her over his knee and smack her perky ass pink.

"Christ, Jules." He ran a hand over his jaw. "Those guns could be connected to other crimes. What were you thinking?"

"I was thinking I needed to protect myself in case someone from my dad's past decided to take their revenge out on me." She glanced over his shoulder, her eyes filling with a sadness that broke his heart. "Turns out it wasn't his enemies I needed to worry about."

"What are you talking about?"

"Nothing." She shook her head and some of the wet strands stuck to the sides of her neck. "Look, I just need to know what I should do. I mean, are they going to do a thorough search of this place, or..."

"They might."

"Shit."

That feeling from earlier became even more unsettling. Though their time together prior to today had pretty much been a whirlwind romance, they'd gotten to know each other well. The important parts, anyway. And even when he had her thinking he was there for her protection, he'd never seen her this antsy.

"What's going on, Jules?"

"What's going on is I need you to help me get those guns out of here without any of them noticing." She tipped her chin toward the men and women outside.

Mike ran a hand over his jaw. "Tell me where they are."

The relief flooding her beautiful face gutted him. "There's one taped beneath the sink in the bathroom in the hallway, and the one downstairs. There's also one taped beneath the coffee table in the living room, and there's a shotgun behind the bookshelf there."

Holy shit. "Okay." He thought for a moment. "Shotgun's gonna have to stay, but I can get the others."

"What should I do?"

Mike pointed to the people outside. "Keep them busy."

"How?"

"I don't know. Ask them some questions. But nothing that will make it look like you're fishing."

"Gee, thanks." She rolled her baby blues. "That helps a lot."

His dick twitched behind his zipper, because her sassy side had always turned him on. "Just make conversation, Jules. Ask if there's anything else they need from you before you leave. Look at the body, and, I don't know...try to conjure up some tears or something."

"You want me to cry?"

"Why not? They'll want to offer you sympathy, which will draw out the conversation." Resting his palm against her cheek, he offered her a small smile. "I'll meet you back up here. And don't worry. I'll be quick."

Procuring the weapons was easier than he'd first thought, since the only other officers left on the premises were the two standing guard outside the front door. Mike even managed to slide the shotgun even further behind the bookshelf, toward the middle where it was virtually out of sight.

The question of why the hell she'd hidden weapons all over the fucking place kept running through his head, along with the fact that she'd bought them from some back-alley arms dealer.

Mike expected that sort of behavior from her brothers or her father. But the Juliet he knew would never have pulled such a dangerous stunt.

Maybe you don't know her as well as you thought you did.

No. This was his Jules. If she bought the guns the way she claimed, there had to be a good reason.

Not yours, anymore. Remember?

"Shut the fuck up."

Great. It was bad enough the tiny voice in his head was right. Now he was talking back to it, too.

Mentally cursing himself all the way up the stairs, Mike found Juliet exactly where he'd told her to be...outside her bedroom, talking with the man in charge.

Swiping a tear from her cheek, she caught his eye as he walked through the open door.

"Did you get everything packed?"

Juliet nodded. "I'm ready whenever you are." She then offered Detective Morales a slight smile. "Thank you."

"You're welcome." Morales shook her hand once more. "Oh, one more thing. When we spoke privately before, you told me the deceased man didn't say anything to you during your struggle. Are you absolutely sure about that? I mean, he didn't give you *any* indication as to why he broke in or was trying to kill you?"

"No." Juliet shook her head. "Like I said, he didn't say a word to me."

The delicate muscles beneath Juliet's left eye twitched slightly. An indiscernible movement to most, but Mike caught it. Between that and his having heard the bastard saying something to her when he'd first arrived, he knew...

She's lying.

"Okay." Morales bought her story. "Unfortunately, the world is full of sick people who do things for no reason other than they can." He shook her hand once more. "I appreciate your cooperation, Miss Farrow. And...I'm sorry this happened to you."

"Thanks."

"Mr. Reynolds." The man held out his hand for Mike, as well.

"Detective."

"I'll be in touch."

I'm sure you will be. "Looking forward to it."

After a half-second stare down, the two men parted ways and Mike and Juliet went back inside. Grabbing her suitcase and toiletry bag as they walked past her bed, he escorted her to his truck.

"Wait." She grabbed his arm. "Lydia!"

"Who's Lydia?"

"My cat. I can't believe I almost forgot her."

He hadn't noticed a cat the entire time he'd been there. Damn thing must've been hiding when he'd gone looking for the guns.

"We can't take a cat to the hotel, Jules."

Her shoulders fell. "Crap. You're right. But she'll be okay overnight, right?"

Before he thought about what he was doing, Mike reached over and rested his hand over hers. "She'll be fine."

Juliet stared at their joined hands for several second before nodding. "Okay."

With a quick text to Derek, Mike requested the former SEAL bypass the traditional reservation route and secure him a room under the name Jay Reynolds. With a promise to explain later, he then sent a text to Jake thanking him for covering his ass with the local cops. He also promised to call when it was safe to talk.

Minus a few dings on his phone from Derek's incoming texts, the ride to the hotel was damn near silent. Not that Mike was complaining. They both needed a minute to process everything that had happened.

By the time they checked in and got to their room, Juliet was wound tighter than he'd ever seen her before. After securing the locks on the thick, wooden door, Mike was setting their bags down when she spoke from behind him.

In a small, frighteningly calm voice he heard, "It's been almost two years, Jay. Where the hell have you been?"

Turning to face her, Mike found Juliet standing in the middle of the room, her hands fidgeting at her sides. Taking a few steps toward her, he locked his eyes with hers and said, "We need to talk."

Chapter 4

Juliet sat at the small, rectangular table picking at the crust on her slice of pizza. After saying they needed to talk—and boy, did they ever—Jay had started to say something, but then changed his mind and decided he should shower and change, first.

Since his leather jacket and t-shirt were both black, she hadn't even noticed the blood that had been smeared on them from when he'd held her earlier. While he'd gotten himself cleaned up, Juliet had used that time to try and figure out exactly what she wanted to say.

Confused and hurt...and *thrilled* beyond words that he'd quite literally appeared out of nowhere just when she needed him most, Juliet had a multitude of questions rolling through her brain. Add to that the fact that she'd almost died tonight, after having almost killed a man...right before Jay *did* kill a man...and yeah. She had no idea where to even begin.

So when he'd come out of the bathroom and asked if she was hungry, she'd lied and said she was.

"You look good."

His words had her eyes rising to meet his. "You look"—*better than good*—"different."

"Yeah." Jay's brown eyes crinkled with his smile as he rubbed the smooth skin along his strong jaw. "Decided to ditch the beard a while back."

Juliet's gaze lifted to his hair. The long, dark hair she remembered was short, now. More so on the sides and back than the top. And there were a few lighter streaks here and there that, when the light landed on them just so, told her he'd spent quite a bit of time out in the sun.

"And the ponytail?"

"Was a pain in the ass." He chuckled low.

Juliet couldn't keep her lips from curling into a ghost of a smile. Having long hair, herself, she could appreciate the comment. But damn, she used to love running her fingers through his long strands while they lay in bed together.

There's still plenty there to grab onto.

She cleared her throat and gave herself a mental slap. Those thoughts had no business playing in her head, now. He might be back, but he wasn't...*back*. Or was he?

Just ask him.

When Mikhail had first introduced her to Jay, Juliet remembered being drawn in by his bad-boy appearance. The ponytail, beard, and tattoos were definitely a far cry from the guys she tended to date.

But he hadn't been sent to her place on a date. He'd been there to protect her.

Of course, she'd argued that she didn't need protection, but her brother had insisted. Mikhail didn't know about her self-defense classes, nor did he realize she knew how to shoot.

Still, even if he *had* known, Mikhail would have worried about her. Because that's the kind of big brother he was.

He'd always been nice to her growing up. Helped her with her homework, let her hang out with him and his friends when she wanted. Because of this, Juliet always had a hard time telling him no.

Ivan, on the other hand, not so much.

Rot in your four-by-six cell, asshole. Right next to dear old Daddy.

A dull ache spread throughout her chest as she thought of Mikhail, again. Sure, he'd done some shady things in his short life, but it wasn't like he'd had much of a choice. None of them had.

But as they got older, it was clear which brother wanted to get away from the Volkov way of life and which one thrived on it. And no matter what Mikhail had done in the past, the one thing that will always stick out in her mind, the one thing Juliet would never forget, was his final act against their father.

The one meant to keep her safe. The same one that got him killed.

Pushing those thoughts away, she returned her focus to the man sitting across from her. His skin's golden tone from where the sun had kissed him was a little darker than she remembered, and with the beard no longer hiding his face, she could truly see just how handsome he really was.

God, he's still beautiful.

The leather jacket he'd been wearing had been wiped down and was now hanging over the back of his chair, and the clean, white t-shirt he had on stretched in the most delicious way across his broad shoulders and taut chest.

Two full-sleeve tattoos were partially exposed, the dark markings looking crisp and powerful beneath the overhead lamp. Juliet thought of the others she knew he had, and just like that, the image of him lying naked beneath her flashed behind her eyes.

Juliet had committed his tattoos to memory, as if they were a treasure map that led to his soul. Intricate and detailed, some were simple designs while others represented specific things. Meaningful things known only to him.

But it was the ones across his chest she remembered most.

Scrolled in the most beautiful font she'd ever seen were the words La Vida Loca, Spanish for 'The Crazy Life'. Beneath that in large, gorgeous block numbers was 1983.

Juliet had asked him about it the first time they'd made love. He'd been open about those, telling her the year was for when he was born and that the saying across it had been added when he'd gotten old enough to realize just how crazy real life could be.

Ain't that the truth.

"You wanna tell me what happened tonight?"

His deep voice broke through her subconscious thoughts again.

She raised an onyx brow. "You wanna tell me why you're here?"

One corner of his kissable lips curled upward. "You first."

"Fine." She sat back in her chair and crossed her arms. "I was doing some work at home and got hungry. I went into the kitchen with Lydia, and I was looking in the fridge when I heard a noise coming from upstairs."

"Is that when you called the police?"

"No, that's when I grabbed my gun and went upstairs."

Surprise left him blinking. "You did *what?*"

"I wasn't going to call the police just because I heard a noise, Jay. I wanted to be sure."

"Bet you were sure when that gun was pointed at your head, weren't ya?"

The snarky comment set her off.

"What's your problem?" She shot up so fast her chair nearly toppled over. "You asked me what happened, and I gave you an answer. I'm sorry if it's not what you wanted to hear."

"This isn't about what I want, Jules." Jay stood, too. "It's about your complete disregard for your own safety."

"My *safety* stopped being any of your business when you decided to disappear two years ago."

"I didn't fucking disappear."

"Funny. That's not how I remember it."

"Please tell me, then." He seethed. "Just exactly how do you remember it? Because what *I* remember is you being dragged out of your home by a bunch of fucking Feds while I was being cuffed with my face smashed against your living room floor."

His voice boomed off the room's thin walls, initiating a few taps by their neighbor and a not-so-polite request that they keep their voices down.

He's right. You were the one who vanished.

That annoying little voice was right. She was the one who'd left him behind. Not that she'd had any choice in the matter.

"Look, I'm more than grateful for what you did for me tonight, and I know I'll never be able to repay you, but..."

"I don't want you to repay me, Jules." Jay softened his voice. "I just want to know why that guy was sent to kill you."

Her gaze rose to his. "Who says he was sent by someone?"

"I know what you told the cops, but I'm not them. I heard that asshole talking to you. What did he say?"

"Nothing."

"Why are you lying to me?"

She bit her bottom lip but kept her chin high and put her hands on her hips. "No. It's your turn to answer some questions. Namely, why are you here?"

"I came to see you."

"No shit. I'm asking, *why*. What happened to you that day, and...how did you even find me?"

"It wasn't easy." He sat down on the bed closest to the door. "After the Feds took you away, they..."

Jay hesitated, almost as if he couldn't decide what he should say. When he finally spoke again, what he told her broke her hardened heart.

"They booked me on a bunch of bullshit charges from way back. I was sent to county and then transferred here, to Texas."

A look of shame crossed over his face and Juliet found herself tempted to go to him. Instead, she sat down on the other mattress and rested her hands in her lap.

"You've been in jail?"

Guilt filled his sweet eyes as he bypassed what she imagined was an embarrassing admission.

"They said you'd been put into Federal protective custody." He shook his head. "Didn't matter what I said or who I threatened, I couldn't get anyone to tell me where you were."

"They took me to some FBI safehouse in the middle of the freaking dessert. They wanted me to testify against my father."

"Why? You didn't know anything about his business."

"That's what I told them, but they didn't believe me."

Because you were lying.

"So what happened after they took you away?"

"They kept me under their protection until the trial was over. Gave me a new name to use if we were ever in public somewhere. For my safety," she scoffed and rolled her eyes. "They claimed it was to keep me safe, but in reality, I was their prisoner. They questioned me nearly every day. About my childhood. My parents. My brothers. For two months, they kept me locked away like *I* was the criminal."

"I'm so sorry, Jules. If I could go back..."

She glanced over at him, the sadness in his eyes chipping away at her anger. "It wasn't your fault, Jay. And neither was tonight." Juliet pushed herself to her feet. She took a tentative step toward him. "In fact, I've acted pretty ungrateful for what you did tonight." Another step. "You saved my life, and I should've said thank you. So...thanks."

"Ah, baby." Jay stood and walked toward her. "You don't ever have to thank me for that."

Her heart gave a hard thump. "Why do you keep calling me that?"

He frowned. "What?"

"Baby." She licked her lips. "It's been two years, Jay."

"Two years." He shrugged and took a step closer. "Two minutes." Another step. "Time doesn't matter when it comes to you. As far as I'm concerned"—he closed the gap—"you'll always be my baby."

"Jay." Juliet's heart began to beat in a way it hadn't since the last time she saw him.

"Shh.." He frowned again. "Don't talk. Let's just..."

"What?" She tilted her chin upward. Eyes lost in his gaze, she whispered, "What is it you want to do?"

"This."

Jay's lips pressed against hers in a kiss so light...so loving...it made her knees weak and her pulse skyrocket.

Two long years she'd dreamed of being with this man again. Two long years she'd spent lost in fantasies of his return.

The kiss started out soft, but then Jay growled as he began to devour her. Just like in those fantasies. But never, in all that time, had she ever imagined their reunion would be like this.

You almost died tonight.

A picture of the man on top of her, pointing her own gun at her head, flashed through her mind.

Jay killed a man tonight.

She could feel the warmth of the intruder's blood all over her face.

He killed a man...for you!

"No." Juliet jumped back, just out of his reach.

"Shit, Jules. I'm sorry. I shouldn't have—"

"No, it's not...your fault."

Her breathing became rapid. Shallow. Her mouth suddenly became dry and a dizzy spell hit her out of nowhere.

"I...I..." Her knees started to give out.

"Whoa." Jay grabbed ahold of her shoulders to keep her from falling. "Easy, there. Here. Let's sit."

"Sorry." She huffed out another breath. "I don't...I don't know what's...wrong."

"You're hyperventilating." Juliet felt his callused hand on the back of her neck. "Lean forward. Put your head between your knees." She did. "Good girl. Now take slow, deep breaths. In through your nose, exhale out of your mouth."

"Why is my...head between...my knees."

"Shh...just breathe with me. In...out...in...out. There ya go."

After a few more deep breaths, Juliet sat up straight. "I feel better, now. Embarrassed, but better."

"Nothing to be embarrassed about, sweetheart." His hand rubbed up and down her back, soothing away the remaining tendrils of fear. "You've had a pretty fucked up night."

Juliet burst out a surprising laugh. "That's one way to put it." Lifting her head, she allowed her eyes to meet his. "I'm glad you're here."

"Me, too." He started to smile but then his mouth fell flat and he dropped his hand. "Shit. I didn't even think to ask. Are you...I mean, is there...someone else?"

She smiled at the adorable way he'd stumbled over his words. With a playful nudge, she said, "I wouldn't be alone in a hotel room with you if there were."

"Good. I mean, I don't want to step on anyone's toes or anything."

The relief crossing over his face was telling. He still wanted her. And, despite knowing she shouldn't...

I still want him, too.

Jay reached toward her, tucking her long strands behind her ear. His lips parted, and Juliet innately knew whatever he was about to say would make her want to kiss him again.

"I'm tired," she blurted a little too loudly.

He pressed his lips closed. With a ghost of a smile, he let his hand fall away and nodded. "I'm sure you are."

Wearing an expression she couldn't quite read, he stood and walked over to the other bed. Not wanting to sleep in the clothes she had on, Juliet got up and grabbed her suitcase.

From the corner of her eye, she could tell he was toeing off his shoes, and when he started to lift the hem of his shirt, she looked away and ducked into the bathroom.

Leaning back against the closed door, she closed her eyes and took several more, deep breaths. He's just a man, for crying out loud. No different than any others she knew.

"Liar, liar panties on fire."

"Jules?" Jay's voice came through the door. "Did you say something?"

Shit. "Nope."

Jumping away from the door, she set the suitcase on the closed toilet lid and began collecting her things. It was only then that Juliet realized she'd forgotten to grab her toiletry bag, as well.

Double shit.

With a quick glance to the sink, she saw tiny bottles of shampoo and conditioner as well as a bar of soap wrapped in plastic. Deciding a second shower would buy her some time before having to face a shirtless Jay, she grabbed the complimentary items and started the water.

Several minutes—and a lot of hot water later—Juliet had actually managed to feel a bit more relaxed than when she'd first stepped in.

Freshly washed, dried, and dressed in her favorite tank and pajama bottom set, she turned the doorknob and walked out into the room. Rolling steam billowed around her, but it did nothing to block out the mouthwatering view before her.

Propped up in his bed, Jay glanced up from whatever he was texting on his phone. As expected, the man was shirtless...and looked good enough to eat.

"Feel better?" His deep voice rumbled low.

Juliet averted her eyes and went straight to the other bed. "I do, actually," she spoke as she pulled the blanket and sheet down and crawled in.

"Good."

Sliding beneath the covers, she closed her eyes, moaning in appreciation when her head hit the pillow. "God, this feels good."

Letting out what sounded to her like a half-cough, half-choking sound, Jay caught her attention with a soft, "Goodnight, Jules."

Juliet risked a glance in his direction, regretting the decision the second she did. "Night, Jay."

If she wasn't mistaken, the browns in his eyes had darkened some, the way they always did right before they had sex. But then something strange flashed behind them just before he reached for the bedside lamp.

The entire room became enveloped in a cold darkness. Closing her eyes, all Juliet could see was Jay's handsome face...and that lickable chest.

She eventually fell asleep to the soft whispers of Jay's even breaths. But later, amidst the plethora of wonderful, sinful dreams, another face appeared.

One hiding behind a black mask. One with the eyes of a killer.

****

Chapter 5

"Your guy's name is Aaron Schreiber. Grew up in the not-so-good part of Los Angeles."

"Record?" Mike kept his voice hushed. "And talk fast, D. I don't know how much time I've got."

Standing outside on their room's balcony, he kept a close eye on the bathroom door as Derek gave him the rundown on the man who'd broken into Juliet's home and nearly killed her.

"Schreiber had a rap sheet a mile long," Derek began. "Started off small when he was younger, misdemeanor drug charges, burglaries...that sort of thing. Older he got, the bigger his balls grew. Did federal time awhile back for a murder charge. Robbery gone bad. Fucker got out on early release two years ago. Played the game, and when his parole was up, he left the state. LKA was an apartment in Vegas."

Fuck. The fact that the guy's last known address was the same city where Juliet's father had run one of the most successful arms and sex trafficking rings in the country couldn't be a coincidence.

Knowing the second that bathroom door opened he'd have to end his call with Derek, Mike asked the vital question, "Any association with Alexandar Volkov."

"As a matter of fact, he was a bouncer at one of Volkov's strip clubs."

Mike closed his eyes and exhaled. "Damn it."

"You're surprised?" Derek snorted. "You really didn't think an attempt on Volkov's daughter was pure happenstance, did you?"

The bathroom door started to open. "I gotta go."

"Watch your back, Mike. I gotta bad feeling this shit with your girl is just gettin' started."

So do I. "Thanks, D. I'll keep you posted."

Ending the call, he went back into the room and offered Juliet a smile. "Three showers in less than twenty-four hours. That some kind of record?"

The question was lame as fuck, but at the moment he wasn't sure what else to say.

She grinned. "Actually, no. Four is the current record. You'd be amazed at how dirty you can get when you're redecorating." With a tip of her chin, the gorgeous woman gestured toward the phone still in his hand. "Who were you talking to?"

Schooling his expression, Mike bypassed the question by giving her a different truth. "Detective Morales called. They're declaring it a good shoot."

Thank God...and Jake McQueen.

Just thinking about McQueen made him want to shake his head in awe. Growing up, Mike had no idea his best friend would end up being one of the country's most influential men among law enforcement. Or that Jake would be his brother-in-law and his boss.

But Mike was damn glad he was all those things. Especially now.

Juliet bit her bottom lip, the simple act sending his libido into over-drive. "So, that's it? You aren't in any sort of trouble?"

"Nope."

"Thank God," she parroted his thought. Her relief was palpable, but then she bit that damn lip again. Sounding a bit too casual for his liking, she asked, "Did he say anything about who the guy was or why he came after me?"

Mike watched her closely, "The name Aaron Schreiber ring any bells?"

"No." She shook her head. "Should it?"

Aaand...there it was. The tiny twitch.

We really need to work on that trust thing, baby.

The irony of that thought wasn't lost on him. But damn it, this was her *life* they were talking about.

Mike ran a hand over his jaw. "I just want to find out what's going on, here, Jules."

Juliet's brows turned inward with an angry scowl. Sounding more defensive than she needed to be, she popped off with, "You think I don't? *I* was the one with that freaking gun to my head, remember?"

For as long as I live, I'll never forget it.

"I'm just trying to help."

The skin on her forehead smoothed almost instantly and she sighed, regret filling her beautiful features. "I know you are. I'm sorry. I just want to go home, see my cat, and try to forget this whole thing even happened."

Good luck with that, sweetheart.

"So let's go."

She blinked. "I thought my place was sealed off."

"Not anymore. That was another thing Detective Morales told me. We've both been cleared of any wrongdoing, so we're free and clear to go wherever we want."

"Wow." Her brows rose high. "That was fast."

That's what happens when you work for a man like McQueen.

"Guess Morales runs a pretty tight ship." He turned and went for their bags. "Come on. I figured we could check out and then go grab some breakfast. After that, I'll take you home."

"That's nice of you to offer, but you don't have to—"

"I know I don't have to, Jules." He faced her again. "I want to."

Biting that damn lip again, she nodded and said, "Okay."

After an hour filled with bacon, eggs, and small talk, they were in his truck and headed back to her house. The ride from the restaurant had been fairly quiet, each one sporadically filling the awkward silence with more random conversation.

"Sorry if I woke you up last night."

Mike kept his eyes on the road in front of him. "You didn't."

"Liar."

There was a touch of humor in her tired voice, but she was right. He *was* lying. Seemed to be all he did where Juliet was concerned.

But Mike knew if he told Juliet the truth—that her tossing and turning, and soft whimpers *had* kept him from sleeping—she'd feel even worse than she already did. So he lied. Again.

Gotta cut that shit out, man.

The voice in his head was right. He needed to quit being dishonest about shit and start telling her the fucking truth for a change. Starting with who he really was.

Soon. I'll tell her soon.

First, he needed to figure out why that bastard Schreiber broke into her house and tried to murder her in cold blood. What happened last night wasn't random, no matter how many times she tried playing it off as if it were.

Pulling up to the curb in front of her house, Mike parked behind her white Toyota Rav4. When they left last night, she'd tried talking him into letting her follow him to the hotel. He'd stood his ground, insisting they ride together, just in case.

If she didn't like the idea of sharing a vehicle to the hotel last night, she was going to love what he had planned for them today.

"Thanks, again. For everything." Juliet unbuckled her seatbelt and glanced over at him. "It seems like an odd thing to say after what you did for me, but..." She offered him a slight grin. "It's all I've got."

"Told you last night, you don't have to thank me for that." Mike pulled the keys from the ignition and opened his door. He stopped when he felt her small hand on his arm.

"You killed a man for me, Jay. I never wanted..." Juliet's eyes glistened as she licked her ruby red lips. "I never thought you'd have to do that. Not for me."

With a look he prayed she could feel to her soul, Mike told her, "I'd kill a hundred times over and not think twice about it, if it meant keeping you safe."

Her lips parted, her sharp intake of air filling every crevice of the vehicle's interior. Not giving her a chance to respond to his bold statement, he climbed out of the truck and shut the door behind him.

After giving her a hand as she slid out of the passenger seat, Mike pressed the lock on his key fob and started up the sidewalk, toward her house.

"Jay, wait. My bags."

Mike ground his teeth together. The more he heard that name falling off her lips, the more he resented the hell out of it.

"We're not staying," he blurted, immediately regretting it. He'd planned on *easing* her into the idea of coming back to Dallas to stay with him.

"What do you mean, we're not staying?"

"Just what I said. We'll go in, get your cat and whatever else you need, and then we're leaving."

"Leaving?" She walked double-time to catch up to him. "To go where?"

"Dallas."

Juliet laughed. "I'm not going to Dallas, Jay. I have a home here. Not to mention my job."

"You also have someone who wants you dead. Until we know who and why, it's not safe for you to be here."

"The man who wanted me dead is lying on a slab in the morgue. It's over."

Stopping just before the door, Mike spun around to face her. "Schreiber worked for your dad, Jules."

Juliet's shoulders shook with a half-chuckle. "A lot of guys worked for my father."

"Yeah? How many of them have put a fucking gun to your head?" She flinched, making Mike feel like a total prick. Still, he couldn't seem to let it go. "You knew Schreiber, didn't you?"

"What?" She frowned. "No. I-I didn't—"

"I saw the look in your eye when I said his name. You recognized it. Question is, do you know why he came here last night?"

"I told you, I don't—"

"Damn it, Jules. I'm trying to help y—"

A loud crash came from inside the house.

"What was that?" she asked in a hushed voice.

"I don't know." Mike shook his head. Reaching for the gun he had hidden at his waistband, he whispered, "Stay here."

"Uh...not a chance." She peered up at him.

Knowing they didn't have time to argue, he let out a low curse. "Fine. Stay right on my six and do as I say. No arguing."

Though she looked like she wanted to say something more, Juliet gave him a single nod. "Fine."

With his gun in one hand, Mike used the other to unlock the door. Opening it as silently as possible, he scanned the immediate area for threats.

The open living and dining areas made it easy for him to quickly assess the situation. From what he could see, it wasn't good.

The place was in shambles. Overturned furniture, broken lamps and picture frames, and cushions that had been ripped to shreds all pointed to someone with a serious beef against Juliet.

Son of a bitch.

Her sharp intake of air told him she'd seen the disheveled state of her home, as well. With a finger to his lips, he motioned over his shoulder for her to be silent as he slowly made his way through the door.

Starting with the main floor, they cleared every possible nook and cranny. Room by room, Mike made certain there were no viable threats there before leading Juliet upstairs.

His rage grew when he realized the second floor was in even worse shape than the first. Especially Juliet's bedroom.

By the time they were finished, adrenaline had his heart racing a mile a minute, and Juliet was still holding onto his belt loop as if her life depended on it. After double-checking the small, partitioned back yard, he turned to face her.

Shoving his Glock 40 back into his jeans at the small of his back, he muttered, "All clear."

Unshed tears blanketed the fear in her eyes. "Who would do this?"

"I think you know who." Mike stared back at her.

With anger replacing her fear, Juliet fisted her hands at her sides and took a step toward him. "My father is locked away in a federal prison. So is Ivan, for that matter."

"Come on, Jules. You know as well as I do that doesn't mean shit. They want someone taken out, there are plenty of people like Schreiber to do their dirty work. Question is, why you?"

"I don't know!" Juliet insisted sharply.

Mike thought for a moment. "Call Mikhail. If your father did send his people after you, maybe he knows something that can help us."

All color left her face, her voice lowering to just above a whisper. "What?"

"Mikhail...you know, your brother? Call him. See if he's heard anything."

Mikhail may be Alexandar Volkov's son, but Mike had gotten to know the guy pretty damn well while he was undercover. Unlike their father and Ivan, Juliet's youngest brother wasn't a bad guy. He'd just never been given an option when it came to the family business.

"Oh, my God." Stumbling back, Juliet dropped into one of the kitchen bar stools that wasn't overturned. "You don't know."

"Know what?"

Juliet licked her lips, those damn tears welling in her eyes again. "Mikhail's dead, Jay."

"What?" Mike could feel his own eyes bugging out of his head. "When?"

"About a year and a half ago. Right after he testified at Dad's trial."

"What the hell happened?"

Juliet simply shrugged. "It's...a long story."

"One that might clue us in on what's happening now."

"No." She shook her head. "It won't."

"You just said he died right after the trial," Mike pointed out. "There's a good chance that whatever happened to Mikhail is related to what's going on with you."

"It's not." Juliet spoke with utter certainty. "At least, not in the way you're thinking."

"How can you be so sure?" Mike pressed on.

A tear escaped the corner of her eye. "Because Mikhail killed himself."

Oh, shit. "Ah, Jules." He went to her. "I'm so sorry."

Swiping the tear away, she shrugged and looked away. "It is what it is."

Unable to let it go, Mike said, "I get that Mikhail wasn't a stone-cold asshole like your dad or Ivan, but he never struck me as the suicidal type."

"Who knows?" Juliet stood from the stool. "People kill themselves all the time, Jay. Maybe Mikhail was depressed. Or maybe he'd finally had enough of our family and wanted out. Doesn't matter now, anyway." Putting her back to him, she made some kissing sounds and called out for her cat. "Lydia, where are you? Here kitty, kitty."

She doesn't want to talk about it, right now. Message received.

Dropping it—for now—Mike went along with the change in subject. "Maybe she heard whoever made this mess come in and ran off."

"This is the only home she's ever known. Minus the shelter I adopted her from. But she was a tiny kitten when I first got her. She wouldn't even know where to run off to outside these walls. Kitty, kitty," she hollered for her beloved pet again. Going to the cabinet near the cat's food and water dish, Juliet grabbed a small bag of cat treats and shook it. "I have something for you..."

"Jules, we cleared every room in the house."

"Cats are extremely intelligent and resourceful." She shook the bag again. "Not to mention Lydia is very bendy."

Mike smirked. "Bendy?"

Juliet's blue eyes met his, humor lifting the cloud of sadness that had dimmed the light there. "You wouldn't believe some of the places she's squeezed herself into." Shaking the bag a third time, she walked into the living room and called out for her cat again. "Lydia! Come on, kitty. Come get your treat."

Worry had just started seeping into her expression when they heard a small noise coming from the overturned bookshelf to their right. At first glance, Mike thought there was no way anything could fit under there. But when a tiny gray and white face peeked out from a gap between the floor and the shelf, he knew his assumption was wrong.

"There you are." Juliet walked over to the timid animal. "It's okay, Lydia. You're safe, now."

As if the cat had actually understood what Juliet had said, Lydia squeezed herself out from under the shelf and went to her. Picking her up, Juliet cooed and cuddled the pretty feline, rubbing her nose across the top of Lydia's head.

Hugging the cat to her chest, she talked to her pet as if she were a baby. "Were you scared? I bet you were, weren't you?"

Biting the inside of his cheek, Mike tried to hide his smile. He failed.

"What?" Juliet caught sight of his grin.

"Nothing." He quickly schooled his expression.

"Do you have any pets?"

Mike shook his head. "My job isn't really conducive to owning a living creature."

"What do you do, now?"

Damn it. He'd opened that particular door without even thinking. "I work for a security company."

It was the standard answer he and the others often gave civilians until and unless they needed to know more. Not that R.I.S.C. was a big secret. In fact, it was well-known and respected by government and law enforcement officials around the country.

But since he hadn't shared his true identity with Juliet yet, he figured it was the best place to start.

Surprise flashed across her face. "A security company hired you? Even with your record?"

Still quick on the uptake, I see.

"You'd be surprised how many places overlook criminal records. Especially when the applicant possesses specific skillsets they're looking for."

Another vague truth. There were a lot of businesses willing to ignore a guy's rap sheet. They just weren't the kinds of places Mike would ever work for.

Eying him closely, she continued to pet the purring cat as she asked, "Do I even want to know what skillset you possess?"

A muscle in his jaw twitched. So did his dick. "I'm a man of many talents, baby."

Heat filled her baby blues as she picked up on the hidden meaning of his words. "I remember."

Momentarily forgetting someone had broken into Juliet's home for the second time in as many days, Mike started to lean toward her. At the same time, the cat jumped out of Juliet's arms, breaking the electrifying spell.

"Guess she wanted down," he muttered low as he watched Lydia take off in a sudden sprint toward the kitchen.

"Yeah." Juliet smiled, the flush in her cheeks telling him she'd been just as turned on as he was. "She's a very quirky cat. At one point, I actually considered changing her name to Spaz."

Mike laughed "Spaz?"

"Trust me." She snorted. "If you stick around a while, you'll see why."

"I'm not sticking around here at all, and neither are you. Remember?"

"I remember you telling me I was going to Dallas. I don't remember *agreeing* to it."

"You can't be serious." Mike rested his hands on his hips. "Look around, Jules. First, a guy breaks in here with the intent of killing you, and now this?"

"*This* isn't your problem."

"Well, I'm making it my problem. And if you think I'm going to walk away and leave you here to deal with this shit alone, you've lost your damn mind."

Crossing her arms, Juliet jutted her adorable chin. "I meant it when I thanked you for what you did, but just because you saved my life last night doesn't give you the right to tell me what I can and cannot do with it, now."

"Whoever's after you will come back. You get that, right?"

"Maybe, but—"

"You're coming with me to Dallas, Jules," Mike ordered the stubborn woman. "Even if I have to drag that fine ass of yours out of here kicking and screaming."

"Oh, is that right?"

He stared her down. "That's right."

With narrowed slits, she glared up at him and smirked. "Well, we'll just see about that."

Forty-five minutes and another argument later, Juliet had packed a few more things and she, Mike, and Lydia were in his truck, headed for Dallas.

While she was upstairs packing, Mike had slipped outside to call Jake. With a quick explanation of the situation, he'd then asked his friend to go to his place and clean out everything with the name Mike

Bradshaw on it, along with anything else that could potentially give his true identity away.

He knew he needed to tell Juliet the truth soon, and he would. He just didn't want her finding out on her own before he worked up the courage to do it himself.

During the long car ride there, Mike had opened his mouth ten different times to come clean about everything. But every time he tried, he couldn't seem to find the words.

The truth was, he was afraid to tell her. He needed her to trust him now, more than ever, so he could keep her close and keep her safe. If he told her now, chances were, she'd tell him to go to hell and take off.

If she did, Juliet would be forced to face her demons alone. No way in hell was Mike going to let happen. So he chose to keep his mouth shut, for now, praying that when this was all over and he did reveal the truth, she'd find a way to forgive him.

****

Chapter 6

Juliet stood in the middle of Jay's living room, angry with herself for giving in. She knew he thought she was just being stubborn, but that wasn't the case.

Someone from her father's organization—possibly even her father, himself—wanted her dead. And if she'd learned anything about the Russian mob, it was that once they zeroed in on something, they didn't stop until they got what they wanted.

Juliet knew she was their target, now, and she was pretty sure she knew why. They were coming for her, and if anyone got in their way, they'd be taken out, too. That meant the longer she was around Jay, the more danger he was in.

Their relationships may have been short-lived, but Juliet had loved him with all her heart. She still did. And if anything ever happened to him...

I'd never forgive myself.

"It's not much, I know." Jay spoke from behind her. "But it's just me, here, so I don't need a lot of room."

Holding Lydia's cat carrier, Juliet glanced around the small space. The two-bedroom house was modest and had a lot of potential, but the décor definitely left much to be desired.

In typical bachelor style, the furniture was basic, and the walls were bare. There wasn't even a single photograph in the entire place. It seemed so...impersonal. For some reason, that made Juliet sad.

Even as the interior decorator in her gave the place a mental over-haul, she turned and gave him a small smile. "It's fine."

"Thanks for coming here." He took a step closer. "I know the situation isn't ideal, but I need to know you're safe."

She set the carrier down and opened the tiny gate, setting Lydia free to roam about the place. Staring up at him, Juliet tried her best to ignore his handsome face and strong physique.

"Why?"

His brows turned inward. "What do you mean, why?"

"I mean, why do you care about what happens to me? It's not like we're still together."

For a moment, he didn't say a word. Jay simply stood there, staring back at her before slowly moving toward her. "There hasn't been a day that's gone by that I haven't thought of you. You're the first thing I think about when I wake up. And every night, when I close my eyes, you're there."

Her heart gave a hard thump against her ribs, and Juliet felt her resolve to keep her distance from this man begin to crumble.

The entire ride here, she'd tried her hardest not to feel what she always felt when he was near. Over and over, she'd reminded herself how important it was to keep her distance. Why she couldn't let her feelings for Jay interfere with her need to keep him safe.

The man was a pure, alpha male determined to protect her. But didn't he know?

I need to protect him, too.

He stopped a few inches away. A muscle in his strong jaw twitched. "There's a lot we need to work out," his deep voice rumbled. "Things we need to discuss. But more than anything, you need to know I never stopped caring about you."

Juliet's heart swelled, its beat strengthening to the force of a kick-drum. But when he reached for her, she stepped back, out of his reach. "I shouldn't be here."

The hurt in his eyes was impossible to miss.

"We've been over this, Jules. I need you here. I need to know you're—"

"Safe," she finished for him. "I get that, and I appreciate it more than you'll ever know. But what *you* don't get is it doesn't matter where I am. If they want me, then eventually, they'll find me."

"No, they won't." Jay shook his head. "I'll make sure of that."

Her heart ached because this sweet, loving man actually believed he could stop the men who were after her.

She needed him to listen. To really *hear* what she was saying. The only way she knew to convince him was to tell him the truth.

"You were right." Juliet hugged herself as she admitted that she'd lied. "Aaron Schreiber did speak to me last night."

Without any signs of judgement or anger, he asked, "What did he say?"

"That my father wants me dead."

He does.

Jay swallowed hard. "Did Schreiber say why?"

"No, but it doesn't matter. They'll keep coming for me, and if I'm with you, you'll be in danger, too."

"I can handle myself."

"You're not listening." Juliet's voice raised. "I don't want to put you in the position where you *have* to handle yourself. But if I stay here with you, that's exactly what's going to happen."

"You're not the one putting me in that position, Jules. This isn't your fault."

"Yes, it is." She walked over to where her bags were sitting by the door. "I'm sorry for all the trouble I've caused, and I will never forget what you've done for me. But I won't allow you to do this."

He was by her side before she even realized he'd moved. "Not your choice, sweetheart." He took the bags from her hands and set them back down.

Juliet threw her hands on her hips and glared up at him. "Are you saying you'd keep me here against my will?"

Without missing a beat, the infuriating man said, "If it means keeping you safe? Absofuckinglutely."

"Yeah? Well, this is me keeping *you* safe." She reached for the bags again, but Jay was faster.

Like a snake striking its prey, he grabbed the bags and tossed them to the side, well out of her reach.

When Juliet started for the overturned luggage, Jay stepped in her path. Then, with a gentle yet firm grip, he put his hands on her shoulders and pressed her against the door.

"What are you doing?"

He moved forward until his body was flush with hers. "I'm keeping you from getting yourself killed."

She should be mad at the way he was manhandling her. She should scream and kick until he either let her go or one of his neighbors came to her rescue.

There were a lot of things Juliet knew she should probably do, but in that moment, all she could think about was how wonderful his hard body felt against hers.

"Jay—"

His mouth landed on hers. The kiss was hard, yet gentle. Needy, yet generous. And it ended much too soon.

"Let me do this for you, baby. Let me protect you." He kissed her again. "Stay with me. Please."

Juliet stared back into his dark eyes. They were eyes she'd always swore she could get lost in, and right now, they were filled with heat and determination.

Despite the situation and her resolve to not drag him into this mess any further than she already had, she heard herself saying...

"Okay."

A hint of a smile was the only reaction she saw before he slammed his mouth against hers.

Part of her knew sex would only complicate the situation even further. She was well aware that there were things she still needed to tell him. One thing in particular that may very well change the way he looked at her.

The way he *felt* about her.

But in that moment, all Juliet could focus on was how good it felt to be back in this man's arms again.

She wrapped her arms around his neck, her hands grasping the hair on the back of his head. Jay pressed his hips against hers, the hard shaft between his thighs rubbing against the ache she felt between hers.

Juliet moaned. Her tongue swirled and danced with his as he continued to devour her. As they devoured each other.

God, she'd missed this. The way he kissed. The way he tasted.

With a growl, Jay moved his hands down to her hips, his long fingers gripping her tightly as he lifted her into the air. Wrapping her legs around his waist, Juliet held on, continuing to feast while he turned and carried her down the hallway and into his bedroom.

They tumbled onto his king-sized mattress together. Using his elbows, Jay kept his weight from crushing her.

"God, I've missed you." His mouth traveled away from her mouth, leaving a trail of hot, wet kisses along her jaw and back up. "You have to know"—his lips brushed against hers—"just because I wasn't here, that doesn't mean you weren't with me. You were right here, Jules. In every thought I had. Every dream I found myself lost in."

Her breath hitched inside her chest, from both his words and his mouth as he brought it to the side of her neck. Tilting her head to the side to give him better access, Juliet sucked in another breath when he gave her pulse point a gentle nibble.

Goosebumps covered her from head to toe as he pressed his teeth into her skin there. A move he knew she loved.

"Make love to me, Jay," she begged. "Please."

In the past, those words would've spurred him into action. But for some reason, when she said them this time, he stopped, altogether.

Lifting his gaze to meet hers, Jay's expression became unreadable. Regret she didn't understand filled his beautiful eyes.

"What's wrong?"

"Jules, there's...something I need to tell you."

A feeling of dread dipped deep into her stomach. He'd asked her if she was involved with someone, but until now, she hadn't thought to ask him.

"There's someone else?"

"What?" He frowned. "No. There hasn't been anyone. Not since you."

Oh, my. "Really?"

"Really." He lifted a hand and brushed some hair from her face. "You're the only one I think about. The only one I want."

The dread vanished in an instant, her heart swelling to the point she thought it would burst. If there wasn't another woman in his life, then whatever he felt the need to tell her could wait.

"There hasn't been anyone else for me, either." Juliet leaned up and took his mouth in hers. "So whatever it is, you can tell me later."

"Jules..."

Jay started to argue, but she lifted her pelvis, grinding herself against his steely erection. "It's been too long." Juliet pulled his bottom lip between her teeth. "I need to feel you inside of me again. Please."

He started this. He'd damn well better...

He went wild, then. His hands working fast to rid her of her clothes. Less than a minute later, they were both completely naked, nothing between them but their own heartbeats.

"You're so beautiful."

He stared down at her the same way he used to. As if she was the most desirable woman in the world. When he looked at her that way, Juliet felt as though she was.

Using the lightest of touches, Juliet traced the tattoos on his chest. "You're not so bad, yourself," she smirked. It was the mother of all understatements, because the man was mouthwatering hot.

His cock twitched between her wet thighs. "This first time is going to be fast," he admitted regretfully. "It's been too damn long, and my control is shit when I'm with you."

Apparently, so was hers, given that a few minutes ago, she was adamant about leaving and now she was lying naked beneath his strong, hard body. Begging him to take her.

But she'd always loved it when he lost control. Loved the way he seemed to let go, losing himself in the moment.

"I don't want slow, Jay." She ground her wet heat against him. "I only want you."

Something flashed behind his eyes, and she was afraid he would stop again. But then he reached between them, lined his tip to her entrance, and entered her body in one, hard thrust.

Juliet threw her head back and cried out, the burning sensation of his thick cock stretching her just on this side of pain. It *had* been a long time, and though she occasionally got herself off with thoughts of him, her vibrator didn't hold a candle to the real thing.

"You okay?" Worry crossed over his face.

"Yes." She rested a palm against his smooth cheek. "But I'll be even better when you start moving."

The smile he gave her lit up his entire face, making him appear even younger than his thirty-six years.

"Far be it from me to keep you waiting." He pulled back, nearly withdrawing completely before sliding into her body once more.

The movement had them both moaning in unison. Juliet lifted her pelvis to meet his every thrust, and soon they found their perfect rhythm.

"God, you feel good." Jay moaned again as he continued pushing himself in and out of her greedy sex.

"Shut up and kiss me," Juliet demanded.

"Yes, ma'am." With a sideways smirk, he thrust into her a little harder. "Whatever you want."

You. All I want is you.

Claiming her mouth with his, he continued to slide his throbbing shaft in and out. In and out.

They kept on like that, the speed and force of their movements increasing with every delectable thrust. Jay continued feasting on her as if he'd never get enough.

She knew the feeling all too well.

Her body began to quiver, her inner muscles tightening around him as she felt him became impossibly fuller. Jay must have sensed her impending explosion because he lifted himself just enough to slide his hand between them.

The man knew her body well—or maybe even better—than she did, his fingers effortlessly finding their mark with ease. Gathering her essence from where they were joined, he began rubbing her swollen clit in small, tight circles.

A band of electricity coursed through her body. Juliet started to cry out his name, but Jay swallowed it with another deep, mouthwatering kiss.

Her tongue licked and laved against his while he continued thrusting and rubbing with utter perfection.

"I'm close," she proclaimed against his lips.

"I know, baby. Go on." His fingers pressed a little harder. "Come for me."

"Oh, God."

"Come on, baby," he panted loudly. "Can't...hold out...much longer. Need...you...to—"

Juliet tossed her head back as she came. A low, keening sound filled the room as she let the intense orgasm sweep ferociously through her entire body. She was so lost in her own, amazing climax, she almost missed Jay releasing his own.

His muscles tightened, his thrusts becoming sporadic and uneven, and he growled out her name as his hot seed poured into her welcoming channel.

Seconds, or maybe minutes, later, she finally found the ability to speak again.

"Wow." She huffed out a breath. "That was..."

"Perfect." His deep voice vibrated through her chest.

Eyes closed, Juliet offered him a lazy smile. "It really was."

Warm lips landed on hers. "I've missed you so much."

She lifted her satiated lids and found him staring down at her with reverence. Raking her fingers through his disheveled hair, Juliet whispered, "I've missed you, too."

For the next several minutes, they continued to lay like that. Bodies still joined as they held onto one another.

What felt like hours later, Jay slid out of her sensitive entrance and led her to the shower to get cleaned up...and proceeded to make love to her again.

As promised, he took his time with round two. Cherishing every inch of her welcoming body until they were both even more satisfied than before.

****

Chapter 7

Mike studied Juliet's sleeping form once more before sliding out of the bed they'd been sharing for the past two days. Technically, he'd shared it with her *and* her cat, but Lydia kept to the foot of the bed, so he didn't really mind.

What he did mind was the fucking guilt that kept pressing in on him. With each day that passed, it was becoming harder and harder to hold back the truth. But he had to. For her sake.

At least that's what he kept telling himself.

His phone buzzed as he was buttoning his jeans, and Mike quickly grabbed it from his nightstand to keep from waking her. Not recognizing the number—and wondering who the hell would be calling him at two-thirty in the morning—he waited until he was halfway down the hall to answer.

Tapping the screen, Mike kept his voice low. "Yeah?"

"That how you answer your phone, now?"

The voice was a blast from his past. And not one he had any desire to hear.

"How'd you get this number?"

Brad Lopez, his former CIA handler, chuckled. "Really? If you're asking that question, you've been out of the game too damn long."

"What do you want?" Mike asked curtly. Nothing good ever came with a phone call from this man.

His cold demeanor didn't seem to faze the man on the other end of the line. "Can you talk?"

Glancing at the partially closed door, he said, "You've got two minutes."

"Sorry, Bradshaw, but this conversation will probably take a little longer than that. Get someplace private. You're gonna want to hear what I have to say."

Shit.

Indulging the asshole, Mike gave his bedroom door one final check before making his way out the sliding door and onto his small back patio.

"Start talking. And cut to the chase."

"I'm assuming you're speaking in a low tone to keep Miss Farrow from overhearing."

What the fuck? "How the hell did you know she was here?"

The other man snorted. "Have you been out so long you've forgotten what we do?"

"I've tried to."

"Right. Look, I get that we didn't end things on the most amicable of terms, but your girl's in trouble."

No shit.

"What do you know about it?"

"I know Juliet Farrow has a price on her head. And after the shit you pulled at her place the other night, Jay Reynolds might, too."

His chest tightened. Mike didn't give a shit if someone was gunning for him. He was ready and would take them out the second they tried something. But hearing the confirmation that Juliet was still in danger left his gut churning and his blood cold.

"Who ordered the hit?" he demanded.

"Who do you think?"

Mike's teeth ground together. "Volkov?"

"The one and only."

Looking through the glass, he made sure the house was still quiet before asking, "Why would Alexandar put a hit out on his own daughter?" When Lopez didn't answer right away, that churning in his gut became even more nauseating than before. "Ben?"

"I'm here," Lopez answered immediately. "Listen, what I'm about to tell you could get my ass fired."

"Then why are you telling me?"

"Because you have a right to know what kind of woman you're trying to protect before you put your ass on the line for her. More than you already have, anyway."

"The fuck does that mean?" Mike demanded of the other man. He didn't know what the hell was going on, but he sure as shit was going to find out.

The sound of Lopez sighing hit his ear. "She's not the person you think she is."

"Pretty sure you've got that backwards."

"I'm serious, Mike. I'm not talking about something as simple as having an alias."

"Then what the hell *are* you talking about?"

"Back when you were working that last case, you were adamant that Juliet didn't know about her father's business."

"And?"

"She lied."

"Jesus, Ben." Mike ran a hand through his hair. "It's been two years. Volkov's gonna die in prison, and so will Ivan. So why are you still hammering away at this shit?"

"Alexandar's out."

The bomb Ben had just dropped was like a kick to the balls. "What the hell do you mean he's *out*?"

"The son of a bitch was released yesterday afternoon."

Mike closed his eyes and tried not to focus on the time he'd spent trying to put those two behind bars. Swallowing down his rage, he bit out a sharp, "How?"

"His lawyer started working on an appeal the second the guilty verdict came down. Gotta hand it to the persistent prick, he's good. *Really* good. Found a loophole that set Alexandar free. Some sort of clerical error."

"What fucking clerical error would put a goddamn Russian mob skin trader back on the street?"

"Don't know, and at this point, it doesn't matter. What does matter is whatever the mistake was, it was enough for the man to be granted a new trial. Not only that, he was also allowed bail. Which means—"

"He's walking around free and clear while he awaits the new trial," Mike finished for him.

He felt sick. As in ready to puke in his potted plants, sick.

Barely controlling his shallowing breaths, he swallowed back the rush of nauseating bile and refocused on the conversation.

"You said Juliet lied. About what, exactly?"

"She knew all about her father's business. Has ever since she was a teenager."

"You're wrong." Mike shook his head." Juliet hates her father and her older brother. If she'd known what they were involved in, she would've put their assess away in a heartbeat."

"And she was going to...until Mikhail Volkov put a stop to it."

Mikhail? "What are you talking about?"

"While Juliet was being held in protective custody, the agents assigned to her questioned her ad nauseum."

"She told me all that, already."

"Yes, but what I suspect she didn't tell you was that those agents finally broke her down."

"Bullshit." Juliet was one of the strongest woman Mike had ever met.

"I still have the signed agreement, Mike. Juliet Volkov Farrow agreed to give a sworn statement against her father and brother. Said she could name names and even give us details of a few deals she'd witnessed involving their sex-trafficking business Alexandar had from one of his Vegas strip clubs."

"You're lying." The bastard *had* to be lying. Although...

It would explain the cache of guns and knives Juliet had kept hidden around her house.

"By itself, her testimony probably would've been circumstantial," Lopez ignored the accusation and continued. "But combined with what Mikhail knew and the evidence you collected, the Federal case against both men was considered to be open and shut. Juliet was slated to testify the same day as Mikhail, but somehow Mikhail found out and put a stop to it. Said he'd retract his statement altogether and lie his ass off on the stand if the Feds forced his sister to testify."

The bile returned. "And they went for it?"

"It was risky. Prosecutor wasn't happy, to say the least. But she was confident she could still get a conviction on both men with the evidence they had from the investigation, plus Mikhail's testimony. So the Feds made the deal and agreed to leave Juliet out of it."

"Jesus." Mike ran a hand over his jaw.

Back when they'd been together, he'd asked Juliet about her father's business. Kept it casual so she wouldn't suspect he'd been planted by the government.

She'd looked him right in the eye and lied. Because she was ashamed? Embarrassed?

Because she didn't trust you.

Apparently, she still didn't.

"Juliet said Mikhail committed suicide," Mike muttered, forcing those thoughts away for now.

"He did," Lopez confirmed the story. "Stupid bastard ate his gun a few days after the trial."

"You know why?"

"Our theory is to keep his father from sending someone after him in retaliation for his betrayal."

Mike hated that, after everything, that's how Mikhail's life had ended. But he couldn't really blame the guy. A bullet to the head was faster and far more humane than what Volkov's men would've done to him."

"Okay..." Mike processed everything the other man had said. "That all makes sense, but why go after Juliet now?"

"Christ, man. You really have lost your touch, haven't you?"

"Ben," Mike hissed.

"Volkov knows Juliet had agreed to testify against him, Mike," the other man blurted what should've been obvious. "He and Ivan both know."

The blood in his veins turned to ice. "How the hell did they find out?"

"Obviously, there's a leak somewhere. Not all that surprising, given how far Volkov's pockets reach. Whether it's in the CIA or FBI, I don't know yet, but I won't stop until I figure out who the traitorous bastard is and take them down."

Shit. A leak could mean bad news for all involved. "Think it could've been the agents Jules stayed with while she was under FBI protection? Or, what about that dipshit, Fuller? He seemed a little too eager the day he and his cronies dragged Jules from her house for questioning."

I'll fucking kill him.

"We're looking into every possible angle," Lopez assured him. "In the meantime, you need to talk to Juliet. Find out what she knows about her dad and brother, and who else she's told."

A sense of dread fell like a lead ball in the pit of Mike's stomach. Looking through the glass, he thought about the woman still sleeping in his bed. He'd been laying there, trying to figure out a way to tell her the truth, but now...

"You want me to *work* her?"

"I read the report from her break-in the other night," Lopez informed him. "The good Samaritan who shot the intruder was listed as

Jay Reynolds. That means, for reasons I don't want to know anything about, you still haven't told her the truth about who you really are."

I haven't told her because I'm afraid she'll never speak to me again. "So?"

"*So*, your girlfriend never actually gave up any useable intel on her father. You have a past with this woman. Use it to figure out what she knows, and then bring her in so we can get a current statement. With Mikhail no longer in the picture, there won't be anything standing in the way of her testifying, this time."

Fear worked its way through him. "They'll kill her, Ben."

"They're going to try to do that no matter what. At least this way, Juliet has a chance to put her father away for good this time. Their attorney's gonna push to suppress Mikhail's testimony. Given the guy's track record in court, he'll probably get what he wants. Juliet Farrow is our last chance at making Alexandar pay for the awful things he's done."

"No." Mike shook his head. "I can't ask her to put herself at risk like that."

"You have to, Mike. You need to work your magic with her and make her see reason."

"Now *you're* not listening," he ground out angrily. "Someone already tried to kill her once, Ben. Then they destroyed her place."

"A message." The agent surmised. "They want her to know they're not giving up, which is all the more reason for her to want to put those fuckers back behind bars."

Goddamnit. "I need another angle. Some way to take them down that doesn't involve Juliet testifying."

"You have one in mind?"

Mike squeezed his eyes shut, let out a controlled breath, and opened his eyes again. "Is the report on Jay Reynolds still in place?"

"Of course, it is. We keep all alias backgrounds active as a precaution in case we need to use them again, later."

"So if someone were to run a background on Reynolds..."

"They'd see exactly what we want them to see."

"Which is?"

"Jay Reynolds was a known associate of the Volkov crew but ultimately served two years for his part in connection to a Detroit homicide that took place a few years prior. Why?" When Mike didn't answer right away, Lopez cursed beneath his breath. "You're thinking about going straight to Volkov yourself, aren't you?"

"Why not?" Mike shrugged. "He used to trust me."

"A lot of shit's gone down since then. What makes you think he'll see you now, after all this time?

"I killed his man. I can use that as an excuse to meet with him. With any luck, Volkov will let something slip about what he has planned going forward."

"Are you even listening to yourself? That dipshit, Schreiber, tried taking out this guy's daughter. Presumably under Volkov's orders. Alexandar knows of your previous relationship with Juliet, and with you conveniently back in the picture, he'll either think you're working to build a case against him or that you're there to extract revenge for what happened to Juliet. Either way, the bastard could easily put a bullet in your brain the second he sees you."

"Maybe. But I don't think he will."

"What makes you so sure?"

"I'm not his target."

As unbelievable as it seemed, Alexandar Volkov lived by a code. He didn't mess with someone unless he had a good reason to. Up to now, Jay Reynolds had never given Volkov a reason to come after him.

Lopez waited a beat before asking, "What's Juliet gonna say when you tell her you went to meet with dear old daddy?"

This next part of his plan would be the tricky. "She doesn't need to know."

The other man barked out a short laugh. "How in Christ's name do you plan on going to Vegas and back to confront her father without her knowing?"

"Let me worry about that."

"What you should be worried about is getting as much intel from that woman as you can. We need names, Mike. People she's talked to. People who were involved in whatever she witnessed back then. If she can give us that, then maybe...shit, I don't know. Maybe she wouldn't have to testify, after all."

"Either way, Volkov will end up tracing that shit back to his daughter, Ben. Don't you get it? *I'm* the reason she's in this mess to begin with." Mike reminded the CIA agent. "If I hadn't dragged her into my investigation two years ago, she never would've been put in the position to testify in the first place."

"You were just doing your job."

"Fuck the job, and fuck you. I'll figure out some way to get to Volkov, but I'm not using Juliet to do it. Not again."

Never again.

Another stretch of silence passed before Lopez spoke again. "You sure you want to put yourself back on Volkov's radar?"

"I'll do what it takes to ensure Juliet's safety." Even if it meant putting himself in danger.

"I don't like it," Lopez grumbled.

"You don't have to like it," Mike snapped back. "You just have to make sure my cover is airtight."

"Damn it, Mike. This would be a lot better for you if you'd just—"

"I'm not using her to get to her father, Ben."

Lopez blew out a breath. "Fine. Make contact with Volkov. I'll have you covered on this end."

"Thanks."

"But Mike?"

"Yeah?"

"Watch your back, man."

It wasn't *his* back he was worried about. "I'll be in touch."

Not waiting for a response, Mike ended the call. He then shot off a group text to Jake and Derek.

After giving his friends the condensed version of this newest development and what he needed from them, he headed back inside the house. Being careful not to wake her, Mike climbed into bed, sliding across the mattress until his body was flush with Juliet's.

Wrapping his arms around her tiny waist, he spent the rest of the night holding her close and praying that what he had planned would work. If it didn't, he knew exactly how their story would end.

I can't let that happen. Not to her.

No, this would work. It *had* to. Because for Mike, anything less than a happily ever after was out of the fucking question.

Chapter 8

Juliet woke to the sound of voices. Blinking the sleep from her eyes, she turned over and found Jay's side of the bed empty. The sheets there cold.

Slipping out from beneath the covers, she scooped a stretching Lydia into her arms and tip-toed to the closed door. Tucking her hair behind one ear, she pressed the left side of her head against the wood to try and listen to what was being said.

Unfortunately, Jay and whoever he was talking with were being too quiet to make out any distinct words.

It's probably just a friend.

Shaking off her suspicious nature, Juliet decided to take a shower before walking out to face the day. Hoping that whoever had stopped by would be gone by the time she was out, she took her time, letting the hot, steamy water work against her deliciously sore muscles.

Flashes of memories from the night before played through her mind. Like every night since coming here, they'd made love as if there was no tomorrow.

Rubbing the suds across her wet skin, Juliet closed her eyes and smiled. She pictured Jay's hands on her. His lips and tongue. The way he played her body in a way no other man ever had.

Another flash hit, and with it came a feeling of impending turmoil. She couldn't quite decipher whether or not it was reality or a dream, but she suddenly recalled Jay snuggling up to her after coming back to bed.

Did he actually leave the room in the middle of the night, or had she imagined it? And if he had, where had he gone?

Pushing the strange feeling that something was wrong away, Juliet went about finishing her shower. By the time she was dressed, and her hair was blown dry, she'd convinced herself to stop looking for trouble where there was none.

After all, she had enough to worry about without creating fictional problems.

Though she could still hear three distinct voices, Juliet knew she couldn't hide out forever. With that in mind, she forced back her hesitation in meeting new people and went in search of Jay. She found him standing in his living room with two men she'd never met before.

They were both tall and, from what she could tell beneath their jeans and t-shirts, as fit and toned as Jay. One of the strangers had a head full of sandy blond hair that looked a bit unruly, friendly blue eyes, and a kind smile.

Standing next to the blond was the other man. He had dark hair, dark scruff, and eyes nearly as crystal as hers. Though they both held the same sort of serious—if not dangerous—demeanor Jay did, this guy emitted a totally different vibe than the blond.

One that told her he was in charge.

With all eyes on her, Jay crossed the room and gave her a kiss on the cheek. "Morning, baby. How'd you sleep?"

"O-okay..." She kept her suspicious gaze focused on the other two men.

"It's okay." He smiled. "I work with them. This is Derek." He pointed to the blond. "We sometimes call him 'D'. And this is Jake."

"Nice to meet you," Derek approached her with an outstretched hand and a friendly grin. His southern drawl was impossible to miss.

With a healthy amount of trepidation, Juliet shook the man's hand. "Likewise."

"Juliet." Jake offered his hand, as well. There wasn't so much as a hint of a smile in his eyes when he greeted her.

"Jake."

She held her chin steady and gripped his hand the way her dad had taught her. Holding her gaze a second longer, the formidable man released his hold and stepped back.

To Jay, Juliet asked the obvious question. "What's going on?"

Giving the other two men a stuttering glance, Jay shocked her when he said, "I have to go out of town. Just for the day."

"Out of town?" She frowned. "Why?"

"It's work stuff. No big deal. Jake's gonna fly with me, but I'll be back later tonight."

"With you? So...I'm staying here?"

Jay's expression turned apologetic. "Derek's gonna hang out with you until I get back."

Juliet looked over at the blond.

"Don't worry, Juliet," Derek spoke again. "Jake will bring your boy back in one piece."

One piece?

She brought her eyes to Jay's. "Can I talk to you a minute? Alone?"

"Sure." He offered her a smile. One Juliet was almost certain had been forced.

Not bothering to make sure he was following her, Juliet turned and headed back down the hallway, to his bedroom. She'd barely made it inside when she heard the door snick closed behind her.

"What's going on?" She spun on her heels, crossing her arms at her chest and waiting for his answer.

His chocolate eyes stared into hers. "I told you. It's work."

"I thought you said you worked for a security company."

"I do."

"It's Sunday, Jay," she pointed out. "What business could you possibly have to do on a Sunday?"

Swallowing, his gaze didn't waiver from hers. "Never said it was a Monday through Friday gig, Jules. Plus, I've been off the last several days, or haven't you noticed?"

Oh, she'd noticed, all right. And she'd enjoyed every single minute with him. But that wasn't the point.

"I thought you brought me here so you could protect me. You said I'd be safer here than in Houston."

"I did. And you are." Jay covered the distance between them in three long strides. "This wasn't planned, and I'm not thrilled about having to leave you here, but it's something I have to do."

Mulling over the unexpected situation in her head, Juliet remained quiet. Picking up on her obvious apprehension, Jay rested his hands on her shoulders and gave them a gentle squeeze.

"Derek's not just a co-worker, Juliet." He shared a bit more about the other man. "He's my friend, and I trust him with my life." Jay cupped one side of her face. His thumb caressing the skin there as his eyes locked with hers. "More importantly, I trust him with *your* life."

She bit her bottom lip nervously. "Promise you'll be back tonight?"

Jay leaned inward, his kiss releasing the delicate skin that had been caught between her teeth. "I promise," he whispered solemnly.

"Okay." Juliet nodded in agreement. Not that she really had much choice in the matter.

One corner of his perfect mouth rose. "Thank you."

"For what?"

"Trusting me." His deep voice seemed to fill her soul.

Lifting onto the balls of her feet, Juliet pressed her lips to his. "I do trust you, Jay. I know it doesn't seem like it since I lied to you before about Schreiber talking to me. I still feel like an ass for not telling you sooner."

"Why didn't you?" There was no bitterness in his question, only genuine curiosity.

She shook her head and shrugged. "I don't know. Knee-jerk reaction from not knowing who I can trust, maybe?" And now that you're back, and we're...*us* again...I don't want there to be any secrets between us. I saw what that sort of thing did to my parents, and I don't want us to have that kind of relationship."

The truth was, he was the *only* person she'd ever really trusted. Which was crazy, since she'd only known him a relatively short while before everything went to hell.

Still, from that first moment when her brother had introduced them, Juliet somehow knew. It was as if she'd been waiting for him her entire life...and then, she'd lost him.

He's here, now, Jules.

Something strange flashed behind Jay's eyes, and he looked as if he wanted to say something. She didn't give him the chance.

Instead, Juliet wrapped her arms around his neck and went in for another kiss. This one was deeper. More meaningful, somehow.

Because you love him.

The tiny voice was right. She may not be ready to say the words, yet, but that didn't mean she couldn't still show him. Make him *feel* just how much he meant to her.

Much too soon, however, Jay began to pull away. When she groaned in protest, his chest vibrated against hers with his soft laughter.

"As much as I hate leaving you..."

"Then, don't," she blurted desperately, then mentally chastised herself. Juliet did a lot of things, but desperation was not typically one of them.

"I have to."

"Fine." She pretended to pout. "At least promise me you'll be careful."

A corner of Jay's mouth lifted into a sexy half-smile. "I promise."

Relieved, she drew in a breath and gave him a playful push. "Then, go on. The faster you leave, the faster you'll be back."

"I like the way you think." His mouth curved into a sexy grin. "Want me to wake you up when I get home."

Her insides tingled. "You'd better."

A tiny squeal escaped the back of Juliet's throat when he snaked his arm around her waist and pulled her to him. She was about to ask what he was doing when his mouth slammed against hers. When Jay pulled away, Juliet was fighting to catch her breath.

Kissing the tip of her nose and then rested his forehead against hers. "I'll be back before you know it."

"Be careful, Jay."

"Always."

After another quick peck, he turned toward the door. He started to open it but stopped to look over his shoulder. "Derek's a good guy, Jules. Don't be too hard on him, okay?"

Giving her a wink and a smirk, he opened the door and walked out of the room. From her spot in the bedroom, Juliet heard the front door open and close, and she knew he was gone.

With Jay's parting words running through her head, she went in search of her babysitter. Almost as if he was waiting for her, Derek was standing in the small area between the living room and kitchen.

"So." Juliet slid her hands into her jean's pockets. "What did you do to draw the short straw?"

One of the man's brows arched high with his unspoken question.

"I'm sure you'd rather be home with your wife than being stuck here with me," she explained, her eyes dropping to the ring on his left hand.

Derek's lips twitched. "Something tells me you don't miss much."

Something told her he didn't, either.

"A product of my upbringing, I suppose," Juliet shrugged.

"I suppose you're right.

There was a stretch of silence before Juliet asked, "Do you guys do this sort of thing a lot? Play bodyguard, I mean."

He nodded. "More often than you'd think. And for the record, my wife understands and supports the job, and I don't consider the task of keeping you safe drawing the short straw. You're important to my friend. That makes you important to me."

Something about the way he spoke made her believe him.

Deciding to make the best of the awkward situation, Juliet passed by him to go into the kitchen. "Are you hungry? I could make us some breakfast."

Smiling wide, Derek patted his flat abs and said, "I can always eat."

Chapter 9

"Thanks for doing this." From the passenger seat, Mike glanced over at his brother-in-law. "In case I forgot to say it."

Sitting behind the wheel of the car he'd arranged for them to drive while in Las Vegas—one with no risk of someone tracing back to them—Jake snorted. "You already said it. Twice."

"Still. Between covering my ass with that Houston detective and now this, I just...appreciate it. That's all."

"Well, like I said the other two times, you're welcome. Besides." Jake grinned. "Your sister would have my ass if I let you come here by yourself."

Mike's brows shot up. "You told Olivia about Volkov? What the fuck?"

"Hell yes, I told her," Jake popped back. "She also knows about Juliet."

Mike fell back against the leather seat. "Great. Now she's going to be worried sick *and* pissed off at me."

He already felt like total dog shit after Juliet's comment about them not having any secrets between them. Now he had to worry about facing an irritated sibling at some point, too.

"Better you than me, brother."

"Fuck off," Mike muttered low. There was no heat in his words.

"Hey, I told you the day I married her that I was done keeping secrets from your sister."

"Um...our jobs kind of depend on secrecy, dumbass. Ever hear of a thing called classified intel? Or maybe client confidentiality?"

"What we're doing isn't classified, and you're not a client...*dumbass.* Besides, I damn near lost Liv for good because of the last secret of yours that I kept from her. We both did, remember?"

I'll never forget.

Mike's gut tightened from the thought of what his sister had gone through a few years ago. Though he'd finally started to let some of it go, the guilt he harbored over that whole situation still ate at him most days.

Part of the deep-cover agreement Mike had signed over a decade ago required him to give up the only life he'd ever known. The government had helped him fake his death in order to solidify the legitimacy of his new identity, which meant the criminals he was after couldn't tie him to anyone but the person he'd claimed to be.

It also meant Mike's sister and father—God rest his soul—had been left thinking they'd lost him forever.

Jake, however, had discovered the ruse when, in a total fluke, his Delta team happened to be working an op that intercepted the same undercover job Mike had been assigned.

His friend had been pissed, to say the least, but eventually agreed to keep Mike's secret for the sole purpose of keeping Olivia safe. Because if anyone had ever figured out who he really was, Mike had no doubt his enemies would have used his sister for revenge.

As it turned out, she had her own enemy to worry about.

While under Jake's protection, Olivia stumbled upon their fucked-up secret. When she realized her brother was, in fact, alive, she'd left the safety of Jake's cabin, and the man who'd been hunting her made his move.

"That was different," Mike scowled. "That was for her protection."

Jake looked away from the road to give him a raised brow. "Yeah? And how'd that work out for her? Or any of us, for that matter."

It hadn't fucking worked out, and Jake damn well knew it.

Mike still had nightmares about Liv being attacked in her own home by that Venezuelan fucker who'd become obsessed with her. He could still see his sister lying in that hospital bed, broken and battered after having been tortured and damn near killed.

The only solace Mike had from that whole situation was knowing Jake had killed the son of a bitch responsible. That and the fact that his and Olivia's relationship had since mended, and now they were closer than ever.

"So, what did my sister say?"

"About Jules?" Jake smirked. "That you're a dumbass, and you should've told her the truth about who you are the night you went to her house."

Mike shot back with a loud, "I'd planned to. But then I got there and heard the gunshots. All hell broke loose, and at that point, I figured it could wait."

"I suppose you haven't found the time while she's been at your place the last few days?"

He started to tell his friend to fuck off again but stopped himself short. Jake was right. He should've said something before now. The thing was...

"If I tell her now, she'll take off. That happens, she'll be on her own to defend herself from whoever's coming after her. I know I need to come clean, and I will, but...I saw what you went through with my sister, Jake. If anything like that ever happened to Jules, I..."

Unable to finish the horrifying thought, Mike swallowed down the lump that had suddenly formed deep inside his throat. God, he couldn't even think about Jules being hurt. Or worse.

His friend slid him an assessing glance before returning his focus to the road. "So it's like that with this woman, huh?"

"Yeah." Mike nodded. "It's like that."

"And you're sure she wasn't involved in all that shit with her father?"

"Juliet's a good person, Jake. The woman doesn't even jay walk, for fuck's sake. She'd never condone the selling of women to the sex slave trade, let alone participate in it."

"But she knew about it. Isn't that what your CIA handler said? She was going to testify, so she had to know something. And if that's true, then she kept that shit from the authorities all that time."

"Lopez says she knows more than what she told me, but I'm not convinced."

Jake shrugged a shoulder. "Might be too close *to* see it. Obviously, someone must think she knows something. Otherwise they wouldn't have tried to blow her brains out the other night."

"Juliet's not the criminal here, Jake," Mike bit out harshly. "Her father is."

"Does she know he's out on bail?"

"No." He shook his head. "I haven't told her, yet."

"Why not?"

"She's got enough to worry about, don't you think?"

Jake rubbed his jaw and thought for a moment. "You got out of the deep cover life for a reason, Mike."

"And there was only one reason I'd ever go back."

A few seconds of silence passed before Jake finally nodded. "Okay."

Suspicion ran through Mike's veins. "Okay?"

His brother-in-law gave him a single, serious nod. "If this woman means that much to you, I'll do whatever I can to help. The whole team will."

Another knot filled Mike's throat, this one for different reasons. "Thanks, man."

"No thanks needed." Jake turned onto another road and pulled the car next to the curb. Pointing at the large gate in front of them, he said, "There it is."

He followed the man's line of site, his gut tightening with what he was about to do. Not that he was afraid to confront Alexandar. On the contrary, Mike was looking forward to it.

It was the thought of facing that sick fuck Volkov again.

Knowing all the shit the bastard had been involved in before getting locked up was bad enough. Knowing Volkov had hired someone to take out Juliet?

He'll be lucky if I don't rip his heart out of his fucking chest.

"You sure about this?" Jake's question tore Mike from his homicidal thoughts.

His voice turned low as he met his friend's eyes. "The man put a hit out on his own daughter, Jake."

"And you're certain Volkov's behind the attempt on Juliet's life?"

"The prick I shot told Juliet he was there because her father had paid him to be. So yeah, I'm sure."

Between that and what Lopez said about Volkov getting a new trial, it was a no-brainer.

"How you want to play this?" Jake studied the gate closely. "Looks like a standard system. We could wait until dark and then make our move. I had D send me the blueprints of Volkov's place, and I found a couple of places that should make for an easy entrance."

"We could do that." Mike turned to his friend and grinned. "Or we could just knock on the front door."

Blinking, Jake gave an appreciated nod. "All right, then. Let's do this."

With a quick facetime call to Derek, Jake was able to unlock the gate and gain entrance into the neighborhood. After that, it was a matter of following the GPS through the spaced-out mansions sporadically located within the expensive-as-shit area.

Mike would never understand why someone would spend that much money on a house that was seventeen times bigger than what they actually needed. To him, a modest home on a large piece of private land was much more valuable than anything he was looking at now.

To each his own.

"There's Volkov's place." Jake pointed up ahead.

Of course, the bastard would live on the largest lot at the far end of the neighborhood.

Mike took in the monstrosity as Jake parked the car against the curb in front of Volkov's house. "I don't see any guards."

"Probably goes against the Homeowner's Association rules," Jake quipped.

"Doesn't mean he doesn't have people watching from inside the house, though. We'll need to stay alert."

"You get my ass shot, Liv will be pissed at us both."

With a chuckle, Mike opened his door and got out. "Just remember to call me Jay," he told his friend. "Otherwise, your wife will be the least of our concerns."

"Not my first rodeo, brother. From now until we leave this place, you're Jay Reynolds to me."

Nodding, the two men started up the paved driveway toward the elaborate front door. They'd only made it halfway up before two men came out to greet them.

Both overly muscular, one man had blond hair and light blue eyes, while the other had light brown hair and brown eyes. Dressed in identical black suits, the two men looked like your stereotypical mob boss strong-arms.

"This is private property," the blond informed them. His expression was hard and his Russian accent thick.

"We're here to see Volkov," Mike responded.

The two men shared a glance before the brown-haired man spoke up. "Like my friend said, this is private property." There wasn't even a hint of an accent in his voice. "You need to leave."

"Tell Alexandar that Jay Reynolds is here to see him. Trust me, fellas. He's gonna want to talk to me."

If there was a leak as Lopez suspected, then chances were good Volkov knew all about the shooting at Juliet's place in Houston.

After sharing another sideways glance, the blond tipped his chin to the other man, motioning for him to go get their boss.

"Good choice," Mike threw out for good measure. Both he and Jake waited patiently, their stances remaining casual, yet guarded.

Men like the one standing between them and the front door were like wolves. If they smelled even a sliver of fear or trepidation, the twisted game was over before it even began.

It wasn't long before the front door opened and out walked Alexandar Volkov, himself. It had only been two years since Mike had seen him last, but from the way the man had aged, during that time, it may as well have been ten.

The man's dark hair had more salt than pepper now, and the lines that had once made him appear distinguished and wise made Mike see him for what he really was. A sad, old man whose best years were well behind him.

"Jay." Volkov's stride was unhurried as he made his way down the curved sidewalk toward the paved drive. "It's been a long time."

"Too long." Mike nodded, keeping his undercover persona in place.

As he got closer, Volkov's assessing glance became obvious. "You've changed."

"So have you."

The older man laughed. "Not for the better, I'm afraid. I cannot say the same for you, however." He held out his hand as if they were two friends greeting one another. "I never liked that ponytail or shaggy beard of yours. Told you they made you look like a thug."

"I remember." Mike shook the man's hand.

"And who is this?" Volkov turned his focus to Jake.

"This is Steve." Mike offered. "Or, as he likes to call himself, 00331984."

Volkov appeared perplexed. "You go by your prison number?"

"Spent so long goin' by it, I hardly remember I have a name."

Jake played the part perfectly, laying the southern accent on thick.

"He's a...friend," Mike informed the older man.

"Ah, a friend." Volkov shook Jake's hand, as well. "Never can have too many of those."

"Another lesson you taught me," Mike commented. Needing to take Volkov's intrigued gaze from Jake's, he added, "We need to talk, Alexandar."

"Regarding?"

"Aaron Schreiber."

Dropping Jake's hand, Volkov swung his eyes back to Mike's. "What about him?"

Let the games begin.

"He's dead."

"And you know this, how?" Volkov didn't so much as blink.

"I'm the one who killed him."

With a schooled expression, Volkov motioned toward the house. "We should take this conversation inside, yes?"

"Good idea."

Mike and Jake followed the man into his home. With orders to remain in the marble-tiled foyer, the two guards did as they were told while Volkov led them to his private office.

"Would either of you like a drink?" the older man asked.

Mike responded with, "I'm good."

At the same time Jake said, "No, thank you."

Pouring himself two fingers of what Mike assumed to be Volkov's favorite bourbon, he took a long sip before turning to face them.

"Now. What is this about you killing Schreiber?"

"He broke into Juliet's home a few nights ago. But I'm guessing you already knew, didn't you?"

"Word does travel fast in my circle." One of Volkov's graying brows rose. "You'd be amazed at what one learns, even from behind bars."

"I have no doubt."

"If you thought I already knew about my former employee, then why did you come here?"

"When I went to Juliet's place, I found Schreiber on top of her. His gun was pointed at her head."

For the first time since he and Jake's arrival, Mike saw a hint of real emotion cross over Volkov's face. "My Juliet...is she okay?"

Like you fucking care.

"She wouldn't be if I hadn't shown up when I did."

Juliet's father made a show of shuffling to his chair and sitting down. After drinking the remaining liquid from his glass in one gulp, he lifted his eyes to Mike's.

"You never told me why you are really here. Why come to my home to tell me something you believe I have prior knowledge of?"

Holding the other man's gaze, Mike had to work hard to not reach across the desk and break the son of a bitch's neck.

"You gave me a chance, once, Alexandar. Gave Mikhail the green light to hire me when no one else would. I killed one of your men and figured I owed it to you to come here and tell you what I'd done in person."

"I appreciate your loyalty and honesty. As much as I tried, those are two qualities Mikhail failed to possess."

"Schreiber told Juliet you paid him to kill her. Is that true?"

Volkov blinked, the look of confusion on his face damn near convincing. "He told her that?"

"Your daughter also told me about Mikhail, Alexandar. She thinks he committed suicide to avoid being tortured to death by your men."

"Mikhail." The man looked away, saying his son's name as if it were a curse word. "That boy was a fucking traitor. Soft and weak, just like his mother."

"Did you order the hit on Juliet?"

Shaking his head Volkov looked back up at him. "You went away for a stretch, yes?"

He's stalling.

Playing along, Mike nodded. "Did two in Federal. That's where I met Jake."

Before they arrived, Derek had worked up a full fake background for Jake. One that included him doing time in the same penitentiary as Jay Reynolds.

Volkov glanced at Jake and then back to Mike. "You got off lucky."

Mike forced a laugh. "Landing my ass in prison was lucky?"

"If it kept you away from my worthless, ungrateful son, then yes. Of course, living off of luck alone isn't enough, is it, Jay?" The other man stood and walked around the front of his desk, stopping less than a foot in front of him. "You need to be smart. And you, my friend, made a very smart move by not falling into the same trap Mikhail did."

"Yeah?" Mike wondered what the hell the fucker was getting at. "And what trap was that?"

"I'm sure you're aware that he turned state's evidence against me. My own *son.* Then he killed himself because he was a fucking pussy. Weak in life and even weaker in death. Juliet is not weak. She remained true to her lineage. To me. Just as you did."

Me? "I'm not sure I follow."

"I had my attorney check the records, Jay. Your name was not listed on any of the court documents. Nor was Juliet's. Mikhail may have chosen the wrong side but not you two."

"That's right," Mike affirmed the man's statement. "We didn't turn on you back then, and we have no intention of doing so, now."

Volkov rested a hand on Mike's shoulder. "Which is why I did not order the hit on my daughter."

Mike studied him closely for even the slightest sign of deception. He found none, but then again, the man had spent his entire adult life lying and cheating to get what he wanted.

"Well, someone wants Juliet dead, and for some reason, they're trying to make it look as though that someone is you."

"You and my daughter...you are still close, yes?"

As close as two people can get. "We are."

"Where is she, now?"

"In a safe place. I have a man I trust keeping an eye on her while I'm gone."

"And you did not bring her here because you feared I wanted her dead."

"You should know...if given the choice, I'll protect Juliet over you or anyone else. Always."

The bastard actually smiled. "This is why I've always liked you, Jay. With you, there was never any bullshit."

"I mean it, Alexandar. Someone comes for Jules, they'll have to go through me, first." Mike zeroed in on the other man. "No matter *who* it is."

"I'd expect nothing less from you, Jay. And for the record, I hope to find the person behind the attempt on Juliet's life.

With a shared look of understanding, the two men shook hands before Volkov led them back out of the office. After a few more final, departing words, they left the estate and headed for the jet.

Jake purposely took the long way there, making sure they weren't being followed along the way. While his brother-in-law drove, Mike sent both Derek and Jules a text letting them know he'd be home in about three hours.

"You think Volkov's telling the truth about not ordering the hit on Juliet?" Jake asked from behind the wheel.

"I don't know." Mike looked over at him. "Schreiber told her as much, but my gut says he didn't do it."

Jake nodded. "Mine, too."

"That's both good and bad."

"Good, because that means Alexandar isn't trying to kill his own daughter," his friend pointed out the obvious. "Bad because if it's not him—"

Mike's gut churned with fear and dread. "We're back to square fucking one."

Chapter 10

"You need any help?" Derek hollered from the other room.

Nuzzling up against her, Lydia's soft, furry hair tickled Juliet's ankle as she stood at the sink washing the last of the dinner dishes. "I'm almost done, but thanks."

"All right, if you're sure." There was a slight pause, and then she heard, "Hey, there's a movie startin' in a few. Looks like a chick flick, but if you want, we can watch it when you're done in there. Figure your boy will be home by the time it's over."

She smiled, thinking Jay was right. Derek was a nice guy. Nice and hilarious.

Between the stories he'd shared about himself and Jay, and his endless supply of dad jokes, she'd been in stitches most of the day.

Somewhere between the first plate and the last, she'd realized that had been his goal. To distract her from the torturously slow speed at which time was passing since Jay had left.

Though Derek hadn't given her any specifics, she'd read between the lines enough to discover a lot about the work Jay and his team did. And what kind of man he was.

Exactly the kind of man I thought he was.

Wiping away the water from the sink's edge and nearby counter, her thoughts turned to the earlier emoji conversation between she and Jay. Glancing at the clock on his stove, she smiled even wider, knowing he'd be home in less than two hours.

It was probably ridiculous to feel happy when her own father wanted her dead. But maybe that was the point.

She'd stared death in the face and survived. Thanks to Jay, she'd been given a second chance at life, and Juliet refused to waste it by living in fear.

With more bounce in her step than she'd had in a very long time, Juliet went into the living room to watch a chick flick with her new friend.

"Okay." She picked up Lydia and headed for the couch. "Dishes are all done. I think I saw some popcorn in there if you want me to—"

The rest of her words were cut off by a barrage of gunfire and the sound of shattering glass. Everything began moving in slow motion. What took mere seconds seemed to last an eternity.

Lydia flew from her arms and made a beeline for the back bedroom. Juliet turned toward the room's blown-out windows, a result of her mind's reflexive response to find the source of the deadly shots. Derek shouted out her name, yelling for her to get down as he leapt toward her like some sort of superhero.

He slammed into her, knocking them both to hardwood floor. Shards of glass and pieces of drywall and wood rained down on them. Juliet heard herself scream—or, at least she thought she did—as Derek covered her body with his own.

The gunfire ceased all at once, and just like that, it was over as quickly as it had begun. The house seemed eerily quiet then, the beating of her terror-stricken heart and Derek's ragged breaths the only sounds she could hear.

"You okay?" A set of panicked blue eyes found hers. "Were you hit?"

Juliet shook her head. "I-I'm okay. You?"

"I'm good." Derek lifted himself just enough to keep from crushing her completely and pulled a pistol from his back waistband.

"Is it over?"

With his eyes remaining laser-focused on the front of the house, he nodded. "I think so, but I'm not takin' any chances." His southern accent grew deeper, his swallow audible. "Here's what's gonna happen. I want you to make your way back to Mike's...uh...Jay's bedroom. But stay low and don't go near any windows."

Mike? Poor guy must be more shaken than he was letting on.

"Trust me." Juliet blew out a breath. "You don't have to worry about that."

"Good girl. Now, go." He rose into a low crouch. "Lock yourself in the room and don't answer the door for anyone who isn't me."

Derek started to turn, but she grabbed his arm. "Wait! Where are you going?"

"Outside. I need to make sure whoever was shooting at us is gone."

"You can't go out there." She shook her head. "What if it's a trap?"

"Don't worry, darlin." He winked. "This is what I do."

Wearing a grin, the crazy man reminded her of a stagehand trying not to be seen as he made his way to the front door. Giving her one final glance over his shoulder, Derek motioned toward the back of the house.

"Go on, Jules. I'll be fine."

Praying he was right, Juliet stared back at the kind man. "Please be careful." Then, doing as she was told, she began crawling on her hands and knees. She didn't stop until she was inside Jay's bedroom with the door shut behind her.

Reaching up, her fingers trembled as she fumbled with the lock until it was engaged. Leaning her back against the cool wood, Juliet closed her eyes and gave herself a few seconds to regroup.

"Lydia?" She made some kissing noises. "It's okay, baby. You can come out, now."

In an Army-crawl move, Juliet slid on her belly to check under Jay's bed. Sure enough, a set of tiny, terrified eyes stared back into hers.

"Come here, girl." She reached in and pulled the shaking ball of fur toward her. "Let's put you in your kennel so you don't run off someplace I can't find you."

Keeping low, Juliet carried her pet over to the corner where she'd placed Lydia's carrier the first night they'd stayed here. It took a bit of coaxing, but she finally managed to secure the cat inside.

With that taken care of, Juliet listened closely for any signs that Derek could be in trouble. She heard none. It was all so crazy...one minute, the place was being destroyed by flying bullets, and the next, it was *too* quiet.

Juliet's phone dinged with an incoming text, the sound damn near making her jump out of her skin. She lifted her hips and dug it out, her heart thumping hard when she saw it was Jay.

He was letting her know Jake had been able to fly a bit faster than planned, and he'd be home in just a little over an hour. Rather than text him back, Juliet called him.

"Hey, baby," he answered almost immediately. "How's everything going?"

God, just hearing his voice was enough to ease her fear.

Juliet had always considered herself a strong person. Hell, just a few nights before, she'd gone toe-to-toe with a man trying to kill her.

But nearly being killed twice in less than a week's time was enough to make even the strongest of women a little shaky.

"Someone just shot up your house." *Damn it.* She hadn't meant to just blurt it out like that.

"*What?* Are you okay? Were you hurt? Where's D?"

"I'm fine," she began answering his rapid-fire questions. "Derek's okay, too. He's outside trying to find the shooter."

"He left you alone?"

"It's okay. I'm locked in your bedroom."

Jay exhaled loudly and softened his panicked voice. "Good girl."

She waited while he relayed what she'd told him, so far, to Jake. When he was finished, he asked, "And you're sure you're okay?"

"Yeah. Shaken up, but I'm good."

"What the hell happened?"

"Derek and I were in the living room getting ready to watch a movie when someone opened fire on the front of your house."

A low curse hit her ear. "Did either of you get a look at the shooter?"

"No. It all happened so fast." Not to mention she was on the floor for most of it.

"That's okay. The important thing is that you're okay." There was a shuffling sound before she heard Jay growl out a muffled curse.

Way to go, genius. Now he's going to be stuck on that plane worrying like crazy until he can get here.

"I'm sorry." Juliet closed her eyes. "I shouldn't have just blurted it all out like that. I should've waited until you got home to—"

"No, baby. I'm glad you told me. I can make a few calls and get some people working on this." There was a slight pause before he vowed, "We're going to find who did this."

"We already know who did this, Jay. It was my father." She spoke woodenly. "It has to be him."

"We don't know that for sure, sweetheart."

"Who else would it be?"

"I don't know, Jules. All I'm saying is we can't just assume it was—"

She screamed and shielded her face as a brick crashed through the bedroom window, hitting the wall to her left before falling to the floor in front of her.

"Jules?" Jay shouted her name.

"I-I'm okay. It was just a brick." Juliet stared at the red block lying a few feet away.

"A brick?"

Though he couldn't see her, she bobbed her head up and down. "It shattered the window by your bed."

"Get out."

"What?"

"Get out of the house."

"No." She shook her head wildly. "Derek said to stay in here until he came back."

"Baby, listen to me. Someone threw that brick for a reason, and whatever it is, it isn't good. You need to get out of the house and go find Derek."

Something else flew through the window's jagged opening. Knocking a large shard of glass on its way in, it landed in the middle of the bed.

Unable to see what it was, Juliet slowly rose to her feet to get a clear look. What she saw turned her blood cold.

"Jules? Did you hear what I said?"

She stood on frozen legs, fear making it impossible to breathe, let alone speak. There, lying less than five feet away from her in the center of the mattress, was something she'd only seen in the movies.

Comprised of a handful of silver tubes and wires, the bomb almost looked like a Halloween prop, but Juliet knew better. This wasn't some sort of sick joke, and the digital timer with less than a minute to go told her she needed to get her ass out of the house. *Now.*

"Juliet, talk to me. What's happening?"

"I love you." The words fell from her mouth as she grabbed Lydia's kennel and unlocked the door.

With Jay still yelling at her through the phone, she ran down the hallway as fast as she could. She reached the end just as Derek walked back through the front door.

Shaking his head with a disgusted look, he said, "Fuckers got away."

"Run!" Juliet screamed.

"What?"

"There's a bomb in the bedroom! We have to hurry!"

Without missing a beat, Derek snagged her wrist and pulled her with him. They ran outside and down the porch steps, making it halfway across the lawn before the house exploded behind them.

Juliet felt herself being lifted off of her feet. The kennel being ripped from her hand.

A rush of heat engulfed her, her arms flailing about as she screamed and flew through the air with a cloud of dust and debris.

Landing face-first in the grass, the force knocked the air from her lungs. She gasped and coughed, doing her best to get much-needed oxygen into her system.

Something hard and hot hit the back of her shoulder just as she was trying to push herself to her knees. Ignoring the sharp, burning pain, she tried again.

"Juliet!" Derek yelled her name from somewhere behind her.

"H-here." She groaned and coughed. "I'm over...here."

He was by her side in seconds.

"Shit." He grabbed the source of her pain—a chunk of burning wood—from her back and threw it to the side. "Are you okay?"

Juliet coughed again and winced. "I think so." She hissed in a breath when she saw a large gash in his forehead and a scratch on his chin. "Are you?"

"Thanks to you." Derek helped her to her feet.

"Lydia!" Her head moved on swivel as she searched for her beloved pet.

"There she is." He motioned to her right.

Juliet spotted the plastic carrier lying on its side. Heart in her throat, she sprinted over to it. Relief flooded her system when she heard the sweet cat meow.

"Hey, baby." She started to open the gate, but Derek covered her hand with his.

"I'd leave her in there. The last thing we need is for her to run off and have to chase her down."

He was right. Lifting the carrier, Juliet looked through the tiny holes to assess Lydia as best she could. She was shaking and scared, but from what she could tell, the animal was okay.

With sirens blaring in the background, both she and Derek turned to assess the damage. The pain in her heart hurting worse than her shoulder when she saw Jay's house. Or what was left of it.

"Oh, my god."

Over half of the roof was gone, along with the front and right side of the structure. The entire thing was engulfed in flames.

"It's me." Derek spoke to someone on the phone. "I need you."

In a daze, Juliet listened as he rattled off Jay's address to whomever he was talking to. Thoughts of Jay and his destroyed home reminded her of her phone.

She immediately began scouring the grass around her. The phone had been in her hand when she'd been running to find Derek. She remembered having it just before the explosion.

There!

Two firetrucks and a car pulled up as Juliet ran to where the phone lay. She picked it up and immediately flipped it over to call, but her heart sank when she saw the busted screen.

"Hey, Derek? Can you call Jay and tell him—"

"Derek!" The man who'd been driving the car jumped out and jogged toward them. A woman with long, black hair much like her own exited the front passenger seat and followed in line.

"Damn, brother." The guy started to reach for Derek's wound. "You okay?"

Derek leaned back and pushed the man's hand away. "I told you on the phone I was fine."

"Thankfully, we were just leaving an unrelated scene two streets over when you called," the woman commented. "That cut looks pretty nasty, D. You should let EMS take a look."

Juliet agreed, but Derek shook his head in protest.

"It's just a scratch, Riley." He blew it off. " I'm good."

The other man looked around as if he were searching for something. "What about Mike? Where is he?"

Mike? That was the second time she'd heard that name tonight.

"You mean Jay?" Derek gave the other man a strange look. "This is his place now, Eric. Remember?"

The man named Eric frowned but then he nodded with a look of understanding. "Jay. Right. Sorry."

"Who's Mike?"

All three turned in her direction.

"Mike is, uh...he's the guy who owned this place before Jay," Derek explained. "And this is Eric, my twin."

"Twin?" Juliet's eyes widened with surprise. With the exception of the striking blue eyes, the two men looked vastly different.

Derek grinned. "It's okay, you don't have to say it. Everyone knows I'm better looking."

"Just ignore him. Everyone else does." Eric—who had short, dark hair and strong, handsome features—held out his hand. "Detective Eric West."

Despite the situation, Juliet found herself smiling. "Juliet Farrow. I'm Jay's..."

She wasn't quite sure what she was. *Girlfriend* seemed strange, but then again, she did blurt out that she loved him.

Doesn't count. You thought you were going to die.

Except it did count...because it was true.

"Jules is under Jay's protection," Derek finished for her. "He had a thing, so I'm keeping an eye on her until he gets back. Shit." He pulled his phone from his pocket.

The detective shared a look with Derek before returning his gaze to hers. "Good to meet you, Juliet. This is Detective York, my partner."

"Riley." The woman shook Juliet's hand. "You know, you look very familiar. Have we met before?"

"Not that I'm aware of." *But I bet you know my father.*

Most members of law enforcement did.

"So what the hell happened?" Eric looked at his brother.

Juliet listened as Derek recounted the unbelievable events, including who they suspected was behind the attack. Eric and Riley both took notes, and when Derek was finished going through it all, Riley looked over at her with an assessing glance.

"That's where I know you from." The other woman smiled. "You're Juliet Volkov. Alexandar Volkov's daughter."

The association with that name made her cringe. "I am."

"And you think your father is the one who tried to kill you?"

Juliet stared back at Riley. "I know he is."

With Derek's help, they went through everything up to that point. Juliet added in how she and Jay first met when he was working with her father before his arrest and incarceration but made it clear Jay had nothing to do with the charges her father and Ivan had both faced.

"Jay's a good guy," she told them both. "He would never do anything like what my father did."

"We know." Derek quickly assured her.

Eric flipped his notebook closed and slid it into his back pocket. "All right. I'll pass all that on with the fire department's investigator. I'm sure his findings will corroborate your story, along with statements from any of Jay's neighbors who were home at the time of the shooting."

"Of course, they will." Derek scowled. "You think I'd make this shit up?"

"That's not what he said," Riley jumped to Eric's defense.

Derek started to argue his case further when his phone began to ring. Pulling it from his pocket, he cursed under his breath.

"It's your boy." He looked over at her. "He called when I was on the phone with Eric a few minutes ago. I sent him a text tellin' him we were okay, but I just realized it never actually went through. Guy's probably losin' his shit." Derek finally answered the phone. "Hello? Calm down, man. She's fine. We're both a little banged up, but we're okay. Eric and

Riley are here, now, and...sure. Hang on a sec." He held out the phone for her. "He wants to talk to you."

I want to talk to him, too.

"Jay? It's me."

"Jules? Oh, thank fuck." He sighed with relief. "Are you hurt? What the hell happened?"

I told you I loved you, and then your house blew up.

"We're okay, but Jay...your house." She took in the chaos surrounding them. "I'm so sorry."

"I don't give a fuck about the house. It's *you* I'm worried about."

"I'm good. Really."

"We're landing in twenty. I want you and Derek to go straight to the hospital. I'll meet you there."

"Hospital? Jay, I don't need a—"

"Baby, I'm holding on by a fucking thread, right now, so please just...do this for me."

The pain and fear in his voice was so real she could practically feel it through the phone. "Okay. I'll meet you there."

He blew out another breath. "Thank you. I need to talk to D real quick."

"He's right here." Juliet started to hand over the phone but stopped when she heard Jay say her name.

"Jules?"

She put the phone back to her ear. "Yeah?"

A slight pause and then she heard, "I love you, too."

Chapter 11

I love you.

Mike couldn't get those three words out of his head. Not that he wanted to. Ever since Juliet had said them, they were all he could think about. That and the fact that he'd damn near lost her.

Again.

Christ, he was getting sick of this shit. Sick of feeling as if he might lose the best thing that had ever happened to him.

And after his meeting with Volkov, he was no closer to figuring out who wanted her dead than he was before.

I love you.

Mike still couldn't believe she'd said that. Couldn't believe *he'd* told her he loved her, too. He did, of course. Had for what seemed like forever. But he'd had a plan. An order to how he wanted things to go...

Keep her safe.

Find and destroy the person or people trying to hurt her.

Tell her the truth and pray she'd understand.

Tell her he loved her and beg for her forgiveness.

Then some fucknut decided to go after his woman and his friend by turning his goddamn house into Swiss cheese, and then blowing it up...with them still in it.

She thought she was dying.

That was another thought he'd had rolling through his mind. Did she actually mean what she'd said, or did Juliet only utter those precious words in a moment of panic and fear?

Deep down, he knew the truth. She did love him, just as he loved her. And now that, *that* particular cat was out of the bag, there was no going back.

There was also no way in hell they were staying in Dallas. Or anywhere close to the vicinity.

"You good?"

He looked over at Jake who was walking as quickly as he was. "Someone turned my house into a pile of kindling and almost killed Jules and Derek. Fuck no, I'm not good."

"I understand why you're upset, but you talked to her, Mike. She's fine."

"No one who gets shot at and damn near blown to bits is fine ten minutes after the fact."

"We are." Jake's mouth turned upward with a smartass smirk. "Like...all the fucking time."

"She's not us, Jake," Mike bit back sharply. That comment was followed by a muttered, "She's better than us."

"The women who can put up with our asses usually are, brother." Jake patted him on the back and smiled. "Speaking of which, there's one, now."

Up ahead, Olivia—Mike's sister and Jake's wife—had just come out of Homeland Security's private medical center's emergency room entrance and was walking toward them.

Before either man could ask, she put up a palm and said, "They're both okay."

"Hey, sweetheart." Jake pulled his wife in for a hug and a quick kiss. "Missed you."

"Missed you more."

"Seriously?"

Olivia moved out of her husband's arms and went to Mike. "Hey, Mikey." She hugged him, too. "I'm so glad you're both okay."

"We weren't the ones who got caught in the explosion." Mike eased from his sister's embrace. "Where is she? I need to see her."

Wearing blue scrubs and a ponytail, Olivia slid Jake a sideways glance. Apparently, the two had been together long enough to read each other's minds because, despite her having said nothing, Jake responded as if she had.

"Yeah. It's like that."

Apprehension filled Olivia's hazel eyes when she looked back up at him. "She's the daughter of a Russian mob boss, Mikey."

"And?"

"And...are you sure you want to get mixed up with a girl like that?"

"Junebug, you know I love you"—Mike used his sister's childhood nickname—"but you know nothing about Juliet or the kind of person she is."

"You're right. I don't. But I do know I lost ten years with my brother, and the last part of that decade was because you were undercover while trying to take her father down. I also know the things he and her brother went to prison for."

Shit. That part would strike a nerve with Olivia. It still burned his ass to know she'd damn near been sold into the sex trade by the fucker who'd abducted her a few years back.

"She's not like them, Liv. Trust me."

"I do trust you, Mikey. I'm not saying she isn't nice, because she seems like a lovely woman. I just don't know if—"

"Then trust me to make the right decision when it comes to my love life. Hell, if you don't want to hear it from me, go ask D. He's the one who found her for me."

"He did?"

Mike nodded. "Ran her background, too. She's as clean as they come, Sis. Doesn't even use her dad's last name because she can't stand being linked to the son of a bitch."

Jake gave Olivia a slight nod. The meaning of which she apparently understood.

"Okay, then." She gave Mike a genuine smile. "Follow me. I'll take you to her."

Turning, Olivia's chestnut ponytail swayed from side to side as she walked back toward the hospital entrance. Mike and Jake fell in line behind her, his nerves firing on all cylinders with the need to see Juliet with his own eyes. To know she really was okay.

As if reading his mind, too, Olivia gave them a rundown of Juliet's and Derek's conditions. Thanks to some paperwork the entire Alpha Team signed when they started with R.I.S.C., the general HIPAA rules didn't apply when it came to them.

If something happened to one of them on the job, they all had the legal right to be told of their condition.

The hospital also had any clients being treated in the ER sign a waiver if they were able, since their physical and mental condition could affect how they proceeded with each particular case they were working.

While Juliet wasn't a *paying* client, Jake had declared her protection detail and the investigation into who wanted her dead an official R.I.S.C. case. Therefore, Olivia was free and clear to discuss her treatment.

"Sophie...er, Dr. Greer...is in with Juliet, now, going over her scan results. Don't worry"—Olivia spoke up before Mike could respond—"they all came back normal."

"What about Derek?" Jake asked.

"I put seven stitches into his forehead and treated a scrape on his chin. Other than that, he's good to go."

"No concussion?"

"His exam came back negative, although he does need to take it easy for a stretch. I'm sure he'll be sore and have one hell of a headache the next couple of days, but he's good. Charlie's with him."

Jake scoffed. "You know she'll keep him in check."

Charlie, or Charlotte, was Derek's wife. She was a super-sweet woman with a heart of gold. She was probably the only person other than Jake who could actually make the dumbass follow doctor's orders.

Another thought hit. One that had Mike reaching for Olivia's arm. "Wait."

She turned to face him. "What?"

"You didn't..." His anxiety roared to life as his gaze bounced between his sister and Jake. "Shit, you didn't tell her my real name, did you?"

"No. I saw Derek first, and he gave me a heads up."

"So, she thinks your..." Mike let his voice trail off.

"Jake's wife. Which, I am. But if that woman means to you what I think she does, you need to tell her before she finds out some other way."

"I know. I plan to."

"Michael James Bradshaw, I mean it." The feisty woman put her hands on her hips. "In case you haven't noticed, Juliet really cares about you. And you and I both know how fast a secret can destroy a relationship. Especially something like the one you're keeping from her."

"I said I *know.*" He scowled. "In case *you* haven't noticed, Jules and I have been a tad bit busy since we reconnected."

Jake coughed loudly, and his wife and Mike both rolled their eyes at the obviously inappropriate move.

"Seriously, dude?"

"What?" The man shrugged. "Just trying to lighten the mood, brother."

Ignoring his immature friend, Mike turned back to Olivia. "Since when do you use middle names, anyway?"

"Why? Did that scare you?"

He gave her a hesitant nod. "Little bit, yeah."

Smiling proudly, Olivia linked her arm with his and the three began walking again. "Good."

"Explain something else to me, Sis. First you're all 'are you sure you want to be with a mob boss's daughter', and then you're razzing me for being dishonest with her. What gives?"

"That was just a test."

"A test?"

"To see if you felt the same way she did. I figured if you jumped to her defense, which you did, that meant you cared about her, too."

"Motherhood isn't just full of wonders." Mike nudged his sister playfully. "It's taught you to be downright ruthless."

His comment made her smile even wider. "I'll take that as a compliment."

After what felt like the longest walk in the history of the world, they finally reached the exam room where Juliet was being treated. The doctor was walking out just as they were about to enter.

"Oh!" The woman stopped just short of bumping into Olivia. "I was just coming to get you. The patient's all set."

"All set?" Mike frowned. "What's that mean?"

"You'll have to excuse my brother, Dr. Greer. He's a little on edge this evening."

"It's understandable." Offering her hand, the pretty brunette woman with green eyes smiled up at him. "Sophie Greer. You must be Mike. I've heard a lot about you from Olivia."

"All lies." He forced out the joke to avoid biting the nice doctor's head off. "What did you mean when you said Juliet was all set?"

"She's been discharged. You can take her home whenever you're ready. Just make sure to keep the area clean and apply the antibacterial ointment I gave her as directed. "

"What area? Ointment?" Mike looked to his sister for answers. "You told me she was fine."

"She is." Olivia put a hand to his arm. "She got a minor burn on the back of her right shoulder. That's all."

"She got *burned*?"

"A *minor* burn. Barely a second degree."

"Your sister's correct," Dr. Greer assured him. "It's a small wound that should heal in no time."

He released a breath slowly and tried to calm his racing heart. "Okay, thanks." With his need to set eyes on her for himself growing with each second that passed, he looked to Jake and Olivia. "I'll find you before we leave."

His sister nodded. "Take your time. We'll be in Derek's room, right next door. Oh and I have Juliet's cat. I told her we could take her to the cabin and watch her until this whole mess blows over."

"Lydia?" Mike ran a hand through his hair. "Damn. I'd completely forgotten about her. She made it out of the house, huh?"

"Apparently, she was already kenneled up, and Juliet grabbed her on the way out."

Good deal.

Jules loved that crazy cat, and—not that he'd ever admit it—Lydia was starting to grow on him, too. If Juliet lost her, on top of everything else, an already shitty situation would be even worse.

Unable to wait a second longer, Mike thanked Dr. Greer and headed into the room. His chest tightened when he saw Juliet sitting there in a set of scrubs, her legs dangling over the side of the bed.

His heart swelled when her face lit up the minute he walked through the door.

"Jay!" She hopped down off the bed and practically ran to him. Wrapping her arms around him, she held him tightly and began to sob.

"Baby, no. Your back." Mike tried pushing her back gently so he wouldn't hurt her, but she wasn't having it. "The doctor said you'd been burned."

"It's nothing." She held him even tighter. "I'm so sorry."

Relenting, he kept her close and kissed the top of her head. "It's okay, Jules. What happened isn't your fault."

"Yes, it is." She sniffed. "Your home was destroyed because of me."

"Look at me." When he tried putting some space between them, she let him. "I told you on the phone I don't give a fuck about the house, and I meant it. It was just a place to store my stuff and lay my head whenever I'm not on a job."

"But—"

"No buts." He cupped her face and used his thumbs to dry her tears. "You're okay. Derek and Lydia are okay. That's all that matters. Okay?"

"O-Okay." She drew in a stuttering breath and nodded. A fresh round of tears hit, each one ripping his heart in two. "My father—"

"Didn't do this."

God, I hope that's true.

Frowning, Juliet swiped at her damp cheeks. "What? Of course, he did. Schreiber told me my father hired him to kill me."

"He lied."

I'm pretty sure he lied.

"What makes you think that?"

"Because I saw your dad today." Mike swallowed hard. "That's where Jake and I went."

"You flew to Vegas to see my father? Are you crazy?"

"I used to work with him, remember?"

"He knew about us back then, Jay. He probably knows about us, now. That's how he knew to send his men to your house."

It was a possibility. In addition to the background the CIA had on file for him, Mike had also made sure Derek temporarily changed the name on his mortgage records to Jay Reynolds. Of course, if someone had been keeping tabs on Juliet, they could've followed her there, as well.

Either way, Mike was going to find the fuckers and end them for even daring to hurt the woman he loved.

"They could've followed us," he pointed out.

"No. You said no one was following us when we drove from Houston to Dallas."

"No one that I saw. But whoever these guys are, they're pros."

"Exactly. Just like the kind of men who work for my father."

"Jules, I know it's hard to accept that someone other than your father is behind all of this, but we have to keep ourselves open to the possibility."

"I get that. What I don't understand is how you can be so sure it's not him."

"My gut says it's not."

"Your *gut*? Oh, god." She went back to the bed and sat down.

"Look, Jules. I saw the look on your dad's face when I told him what Schreiber said to you. He had no idea what that asshole was talking about. And when he talked about finding whoever was behind all this, let's just say he seemed pretty damn eager to beat me to the punch."

Her tear-filled eyes rose to meet his, and Mike wished like hell he could take away the pain and fear he saw there.

"If that's true"—she spoke almost as if she were in a daze—"if he isn't the one trying to kill me, then who is? And why do they want me dead?"

"I don't know, but I swear to you, I'm going to find out."

"How?" Juliet's long, dark hair brushed across her shoulders and back when she shook her head. "If it's really not my father, that means it could be...anyone."

Mike went to her. He took her hand in his, treading carefully with his words. As much as he wanted to spill his guts, she was much too vulnerable to do it, now.

"I know. But, sweetheart, the team I work for is the best in the business. This is what we do, so if anyone can find the person responsible for all of this, it's them."

She sat there for a moment, processing everything he'd said before she asked, "So, what do we do until then?"

"I want to take you away from here."

"Great." Juliet slid from the mattress and walked around him to the other side of the room. "So we go somewhere else until when? They find us there like they did here? And after that, we'll be forced to go to yet another place, and another..." She shook her head and crossed her arms. "I don't want to keep running all over the damn country, Jay."

"We won't." He covered the small space between them. "As soon as we landed, I made a phone call. There's a place we can go. A cabin in Colorado."

Her blue eyes grew wide. "Colorado?"

"It's secluded and secure. A hundred acres surrounded by a high-powered, electrical fence. It's located in a valley with nothing around but mountains and wilderness for miles."

Mike could tell she still wasn't convinced, so he stepped closer, took her face between his palms, and tipped her head up so she was looking back at him.

He needed to look into her eyes when he said this next part.

"I don't know about you, but I meant what I said tonight. I love you, Juliet. I think I have from that first moment I laid eyes on you."

She blinked, a single tear escaping down her cheek and landing on his hand. "I love you, too, J—"

Mike took her mouth in his, the kiss swallowing that godforsaken name. Hearing her say she loved him was the best sound in the world, but it tore him to shreds knowing she was in love with someone who didn't even exist.

When we get to the cabin...that's when I'll tell her.

Shitty situation or not, the guilt was eating him alive from the in-side out. The longer he waited, the harder it was going to be. Juliet didn't deserve that.

I don't deserve her.

Resting his forehead against hers, he whispered, "I need you safe, baby."

"What about you?" She looked up at him. "You shouldn't have to stop living your life just to protect me."

"Don't you get it? Baby, *you* are my life. My everything."

Juliet was his. His to love. His to cherish. And his to protect with everything he had.

Another tear fell when she nodded. "Call your friend. Tell him we're coming to Colorado."

Chapter 12

Juliet sat on the large, flat rock and stared out over the water. Crisp and blue, the small river flowed at a soothing pace as a cool breeze blew through her hair.

Lifting her gaze higher, she took in the entire scene. The tall, thick evergreens lining both sides of the river seemed to go on forever. The mountains' jagged and gentle slopes resting against the beautiful horizon.

Quiet and peaceful, it was picture-perfect. Truly the most beautiful place she'd ever seen. Too bad it was her personal prison.

"It's starting to get pretty cold," Jay said from his spot beside her. "We should probably head back to the cabin before long."

Jake had flown them to Colorado late last night...on his private jet. Juliet still couldn't believe he owned one. She also was shocked to discover that—in addition to being Jay's childhood friend—he was Jay's boss who also happened to own the whole freaking company.

It didn't matter to her one way or the other. By the time they left the hospital and boarded the jet, she was dead on her feet—no pun intended—and within minutes of taking air, she was out like a light.

It was too dark to see much of anything when they'd landed, but this morning, after checking to make sure the immediate area around the cabin was as secure as Jay's friend had claimed, he'd deemed it safe enough to go for a short walk.

"It's gorgeous here," she spoke wistfully. "So quiet and peaceful. It's almost feels like we're in a completely different world than the one we live in."

"I agree." Jay wrapped an arm around her shoulders and pulled her close. "I could stay right here with you and be perfectly content."

She could almost envision a life like that. She and Jay living in a quaint, quiet cabin in the woods. No one around to bother them or recognize her. Somewhere she could spend all day, every day just...being.

I want that life, someday. I want that life with him.

"Come on." He pushed himself to his feet and then held out a hand. "Let's get back before a bear decides to wander up here and have us for dinner."

"Thanks for that lovely image." Juliet chuckled as she accepted his help. "Speaking of dinner, what sounds good to you?"

"I don't know. Ben stocked the fridge and cupboards before we got here, so there should be a good variety of things. Why don't you pick?"

"Oh, no. *I* chose breakfast and lunch. This meal's all you." When Jay smiled, she asked him, "What?"

"Just seems funny. Last night you were dodging bullets and bombs, and today we're arguing over who's gonna choose what we eat for dinner."

Juliet felt her smile falter a little. She'd done her best to push away the events of the previous night. It hadn't really worked, but that hadn't stopped her from trying.

"Sorry. I shouldn't have brought it up."

"It's okay. I mean, it is what it is, right?"

Walking with Jay's arm around her shoulders like before, Juliet leaned into him, soaking up every ounce of his warm embrace. She felt him kiss the top of her head through her hat. A hat that his friend Ben had purchased for her—along with a whole slew of clothing and other necessities.

She couldn't believe the lengths the mysterious man had gone to in order to ensure she and Jay were comfortable and taken care of. In her world, or more accurately, her father's world, no one ever did anything for someone else unless they expected payment in return.

Sometimes that payment came in the form of cash. Sometimes in a beat-down. Then there were the other times...the ones Juliet never saw but heard whispers about. Those were the things of real nightmares.

But Jay had assured her this Ben guy was totally on the up-and-up, and she trusted him, so...

The thought left her smiling.

"Do I even want to know what's going on in that pretty head of yours?"

She glanced up at Jay whose mouth was curled into that half-smile she'd grown to love. Her lower half tingled the way it always did when he looked at her like that, and suddenly nightmares and boogie men were the farthest thing from her mind.

"I was just thinking how soft that rug in front of the fireplace looked."

Heat filtered behind his eyes. "Oh, yeah?"

She nodded. "Maybe when we get inside, we should check it out. See just how comfortable it is."

"I've said it before, woman. I love the way you think."

"In that case, I think the last one there has to...wash the dinner dishes!"

Running as fast as she could in her new hiking boots, Juliet slipped out from under his arm and took off for the cabin.

"Hey!" Jay began running after her. "Cheaters never win!"

She laughed and stole a glance from over her shoulder. "That's what you think!"

He caught up to her in the end, but she didn't mind. Juliet did, however, learn that the rug in question was every bit as soft as it looked.

Three days later, they were still living the dream...if the dream was to hide out away from civilization while Jay and his team back home tried to figure out who wanted her dead.

Still, as far as safe houses went, this one was a hell of a lot better than the one she'd been forced to stay in two years before.

Juliet glanced at the man sitting across from her and smiled. Yes, this one was much, *much* better.

"Well...lunch is over. Whatever will we do, now?" She straightened her leg and ran her socked foot up and down the bottom of his denim-covered calf.

Looking much too serious for her liking, Jay stood and picked up their plates and silverware. "Saw on the news that a storm's supposed to come through here in the next couple of days. I need to go chop some more wood before it hits."

Blinking at his suddenly strange demeanor, Juliet glanced over at the ample stack of wood by the fireplace. "You need more?"

He set the dishes in the sink and headed for the door. Grabbing his coat and hat from the wooden peg near hers, he shook his head. "That won't last us a full day."

"What about the massive stack on the porch? Won't that be enough?"

"Not if we get snowed in for a significant period of time." He threw on his cap and gloves. "Stay inside. Don't—"

"Answer the door unless it's you. I know the drill, Jay."

Something strange—almost angry—flashed behind his eyes. "I'll be back in a little while."

And with that, he was gone.

What the...

Juliet's mind began to race through the past few days. Had she done or said something to upset him?

She couldn't think of a single thing that had existed between them that wasn't warm, loving, or passionate.

Maybe he was worried because his team hadn't figured out who wanted her dead yet. That had to be it because nothing else made sense.

Despite his rules, Juliet rushed to put on her boots and grabbed her coat. She needed to go to him. To let him know everything would be okay.

Maybe it was this place. Or more likely, the man she'd been sharing the place with. Either way, she'd finally started to believe that to be true.

Somehow, some way, they were going to get through this mess. After that, they'd finally be free to start the life they both wanted...together.

Juliet turned the knob and opened the door, letting out a tiny squeal of surprise when she saw a man standing in front of her. He was tall and lean, his dark hair parted perfectly to one side. And his gloved hand was raised into a fist, as if he'd been about to knock.

"You must be Juliet. I'm sorry I startled you."

He knows my name.

Her heart began to race. She should slam the door and lock it, but instead, Juliet found herself asking, "W-who are you?"

"My apologies. I'm Ben. This is my cabin."

"Show me some I.D."

Despite the harshness of her order, the man's thin lips curved into an approving grin. "I see your protector has trained you well. Here." He pulled out his wallet and flipped it open for her.

Juliet studied it closely, her mouth dropping when she read his credentials. "Your CIA?"

"I am. But if you tell anyone, I'll have to kill you."

Her eyes flew up to his, which were filled with humor.

"Sorry." Ben offered her a chagrined smirk. "That joke was in poor taste, given the circumstances." A bout of awkward silence filled the air between them before he said, "Glad to see the boots fit. I hope the fuzzy black slippers I picked out for you do, as well."

Okay, he must be legit. Otherwise, how would he know about the slippers?

"Everything was perfect. Thank you."

"You're welcome."

When he didn't say anything more, she asked, "Is there something I can help you with?"

"I just came to drop this off." He held up a folder she hadn't even noticed before then. "Is your man here? There's some intel in here I think he's going to be interested in."

"Is that about my case?" Hope bloomed inside her chest. "Do you know who's been trying to hurt me?"

"We might. We've recently come across a couple new leads. That's why I wanted to bring this to you both now, rather than wait. With the snowstorm coming, I was afraid the phone lines would be down, and I wouldn't be able to email or fax it later."

Excited to see what was in it, Juliet took the folder and said, "Jay's out cutting wood, but I'll make sure he gets it."

A strange expression fell over the man, but it was gone in a flash. "Excellent. Please see that he does." He glanced up at the gray sky. "I'd better be going. I'm sure you two wouldn't enjoy having a third wheel stuck up here with you."

Juliet wasn't quite sure how to respond to that, so she simply smiled.

"Take care, Miss Farrow. Make sure Mik...er, *Jay*...gets that as soon as possible."

Did he almost say Mike?

A gnawing feeling crept deep into her gut.

"Thank you."

Ben turned to leave, and Juliet quickly shut the door and locked it. Rushing back over to the table, she sat down and opened the folder. That feeling worsened when she read the words on the very first page.

There, in bold print, the sheet read...

Classified.

Property of the CIA

For CIA Paramilitary Operations Officer Michael J. Bradshaw's Eyes Only.

Michael J. Bradshaw...Michael Bradshaw...Mike.

"Oh, my god."

Juliet's hand flew to her mouth, her throat working to keep the bile rushing up from her stomach at bay.

No, no, no.

She shot up from the chair and went to the kitchen sink. Clamping her fingers around its edge, she squeezed until her knuckles turned white.

Was it possible? Could Jay really be an undercover agent with the CIA?

Her mind raced as it attempted to go back over their time spent together. Back to two years ago...and now.

She'd met him through her brother, Mikhail. The same brother who, not long after, testified against their father and other brother.

When she'd been taken into custody, he vanished without a trace. She'd even tried looking him up once the trial was over, but the one measly trail she'd found had led to a dead end.

Then, out of nowhere, he shows up suddenly. At the exact moment a man from her father's past had tried to kill her. He'd rushed in, saved the day, and she'd fallen for the ruse like a mindless damsel in distress.

Jay...Mike...had questioned her that next day after they'd gone to her place. She thought he was trying to help her, but looking back, Juliet could see it for what it really was.

He'd been interrogating me. Gathering information for the CIA.

A memory from the night of the explosion surfaced. One from when she and Derek were on the floor taking fire.

I want you to make your way back to Mike's...uh...Jay's bedroom. But stay low, and don't go near any windows.

At the time, she thought he'd misspoken by telling her to go to his room. But now...

Another memory struck. One with Derek's brother, Eric.

What about Mike? Where is he?

Derek had played it off, reminding his brother that 'Mike' was the name of the man who'd owned the home previously.

"And I bought it," she whispered to herself.

Jay's...no, *Mike's* words from that night at the hospital hit her like a kick to the gut...

I meant what I said tonight. I love you, Juliet. I think I have from that first moment I laid eyes on you.

"Oh, god." Juliet felt sick in the deepest parts of her soul. "I bought it all."

Losing the battle, she doubled over and vomited into the sink. Her stomach didn't stop convulsing until it was depleted of every last ounce of the lunch they'd just shared.

Trembling, she rinsed out the sink and ran the garbage disposal, and on wooden legs she made her way back to the bathroom. There, she brushed her teeth and gargled with mouthwash to rid herself of the rancid taste, wishing she could get rid of the overwhelming feeling of betrayal just as easily.

When she was finished, she went back to the front room and took off her coat and gloves. Shoving the gloves into the pockets, she hung the coat on her peg and went back to the table where she'd been sitting.

Removing the paper with Mike's *real* name, she closed the folder and placed the paper neatly on top. Then...she waited.

A very long, torturous forty-five minutes later, he came back. "Damn, it's getting cold out there."

Not as cold as it's about to get in here.

Juliet remained silent.

The man she'd known as Jay—the same man she'd given her body, heart, and soul to—glanced up at her and frowned.

"Listen, Jules. We need to talk."

Ya think?

He ran a hand through his hair. "There's something..." His chest rose and fell with a long, deep breath. "There's something I need to tell you. Something I should've told you a long damn time ago, but I—"

"Ben stopped by," she cut him off. The jerk had stolen her heart. Her *trust*. She wasn't going to give him the satisfaction of taking this moment from her, too.

"Ben?" Jay's—no, *Mike's*—frown deepened. "What did he want? And why the hell did you answer the door for him?"

"I didn't," she spoke coldly. "I opened the door to go find you, and found him standing there, instead."

Confused, he turned and hung up his things. "It's his place, so he has the code to the gate at the property line. Explains why my sensor didn't go off when the gate opened." He turned back around. "What did he want?"

"To give you this." She pushed the folder...and the paper...toward him.

"What is it?"

"I don't know. You tell me, *Mike*."

His brown eyes shot to hers. The color drained from his face, and...there it was. Confirmation that her suspicion was spot on.

"Jules, I can—"

"Explain?" She huffed out a humorless laugh. "Oh, you bet your lying ass, you're gonna explain. And when you're finished, you can call Jake, or whatever the hell his name is, and tell him to get his goddamn jet back here and take me home."

Chapter 13

I've lost her.

Juliet was sitting less than five feet away from him, but in that moment, it felt as if an entire world separated them.

She hates me.

No, this was worse than hate. The woman he loved and cherished, the one he wanted to spend the rest of his life with, was staring back at him as if he were a stranger.

He couldn't even be mad about it because, to her, that was exactly what he was. A stranger. Except he wasn't.

What Juliet didn't know—what she couldn't possibly see through the blinding haze of anger and betrayal currently surrounding her—was that when he was with her, Mike felt more like his true self than ever before.

With her, Mike was...home.

It wasn't a conscious effort on his part. At first, he'd done everything he could to fight against the magnetic pull the incredible woman held over him. But it didn't matter.

From damn near the first minute they'd met, Juliet Farrow had somehow broken through his barriers. She brought out the best of him, and Mike was defenseless against her.

And now, thanks to Ben Lopez, he'd lost her.

If he hadn't come by with that goddamn folder, Mike would've had the chance to tell her himself.

You had your chance. You had a fuckton of chances. You blew this, dipshit. No one else. Now you have to try and make it right.

Staring back at her, Mike tried to explain. "Look, Jules. I know this looks bad. But if you'll just let me—"

"Bad?" Juliet pulled her gaze from his and laughed. "Oh, this is way worse than bad. This is..." She shook her head and rose to her feet. "I can't even find the word to describe what this is."

"I wanted to tell you. Hell, this is what I came back in to tell you!"

"Yeah? Why, now? We've spent all this time together...first at your place and then here. You've had ample opportunity to come clean, Ja...Mike." She raked her fingers through her long hair. "But you never said a fucking word. But then your buddy, Ben, drops this bomb in my lap, and you just happen to pick that moment to tell me the truth. Do I look that fucking stupid to you?"

"No." He took a step forward. Juliet put out a hand and stepped backward. "Damn it, Jules. Keeping this shit from you has been *killing* me. I fucking hated doing it two years ago, and it's been even harder since I found you, again."

"I'm so sorry this has been so hard for you."

"No, that's not what I—"

"This is unbelievable." She put both hands on the top of her head. "I trusted you. Actually trusted you. I slept with you, for Christ's sake. I thought I...I told you I..."

"Love me. You do, baby. And I love you."

"I don't even know who you are!" She threw her hands to the side and shouted. "How the hell can I love somebody I don't even know?"

Shit. Fuck. Shit!

"You know me, Jules. Yeah, I may have lied about my name and what I did for a living, but you know me. The important parts...the real parts. The part of me that loves you more than anything in this entire fucking world."

"No." Juliet shook her head sadly. "I don't."

"Yes, you do."

Mike went to her, then. He wanted so badly to take her hands in his, but knew she'd probably deck him if he tried. So he just stood there, in front of her, begging her to believe him.

"Everything about us is real." He stared into her sad, beautiful eyes. "Everything I said about you and me...about loving you. That's real. Always."

"How can I possibly know that?"

"Because it's the truth."

"The truth," she scoffed. "You've been lying to me from the second we met. I know nothing about you...Michael J. Bradshaw."

His name left her lips in a sarcastic quip of anger and disgust, and Mike felt as though his entire world was imploding around him. He was drowning in a sea of deceit and lies. A sea he, himself, had created two years ago.

And there was no life raft in sight.

"What do you want to know?" He refused to let go of the dream. Of her. "Ask me anything you want, and I will tell you the God's honest truth."

"Right."

"I'm serious, Juliet. It doesn't matter what it is...good, bad, embarrassing, ugly...I'll tell you everything."

Her inner turmoil was a living, breathing thing. Mike knew she wanted nothing more than to tell him to go to hell and storm out. Thankfully, however, their secluded location was on his side.

It was the *only* thing he had going for him.

"Fine." Juliet walked back over to the table and sat down. "I don't know why I'm wasting my time, but sure, I'll play along. But so help me God, if I even think you're lying to me, I'll walk out that door and take my chances with the fucking bears."

If he wasn't balls-deep in trouble with the spitfire woman, he would've smiled. But this was it. His one and only chance to make her understand, and there was no room for error.

Feeling as if he were in the fight of his life, Mike took a seat in the chair directly across from her. Willing to let her interrogate him for as long as it took, he rested his elbows on the table and said, "What is it you want to know?"

"Is your name really Michael Bradshaw?"

"Yes."

"Do you really work for the CIA?"

"No." When her brows turned inward, he quickly added, "But I used to. I work for a private security company called R.I.S.C. The acronym stands for recue, intel, security, and capture. We're basically a privately-owned black ops team, but we also work with different government agencies from time to time."

"Were you working for the CIA when we met?"

"Yes." He swallowed, then voluntarily offered up more about his past. "I was in the military before that. Delta Force. Jake and I were on the same team."

"So, his name really is Jake?"

"Yes."

"But you didn't grow up together."

"We did. I've known him since we were kids. Jake, my sister, and I used to always hang out together. Then, we grew up, and he married my sister."

"Your sister?" She blinked again. "I thought he was married to the nurse who took care of me." Mike opened his mouth to explain, but she figured it out before he got the chance. "Oh. Right. I can see it, now. The resemblance."

The corners of Mike's lips rose slightly. "Olivia's my little sister."

"She seemed...nice. Then again, she didn't bother to tell me the truth either, so..."

"Because she knew I needed to tell you myself. And for the record, she gave me a royal ass-chewing that night at the hospital."

"Why?"

"When Liv found out you and I were...together...she reamed my ass up one side and down the other for lying to you."

Juliet sat back in her chair. "Nice to see at least one Bradshaw has a set of balls."

Mike did smile, then. Just a tiny one that fell almost as quickly as it had risen. "Anyway, after high school, Jake and I joined the Army. We went to Ranger school together, and then we were assigned to the same Delta team."

"Delta...that's like special ops, right?"

"It is. We served together right up until the day a man from the CIA visited me. Took me behind closed doors, told me they needed me for a special undercover assignment. Apparently, they'd worked it all out with my CO, and the paperwork for early release from my military contract had already been approved. They just needed me to agree to it."

"And?"

"And...I did. It wasn't your run-of-the-mill cover assignment, though. It was especially dangerous."

"How so?"

"The man we were after would make your dad and Ivan look like a couple of teddy bears. And they had arms that reached all over the world. Because of this, the CIA said I needed to take every precaution I could to protect my family."

"What did you do?"

"I let everyone I knew and loved think I was dead. My dad and sister...Jake. They were all told I'd been killed in a training accident. It was supposed to be temporary...a month-long assignment. Two at the most."

"How long did it actually last?"

"Ten years."

"Ten years?" Juliet sat straight up. "You let your family think you were dead for an entire decade?"

"I didn't have a choice. They fucked me over with some bullshit clause in my contract I didn't know existed. One that stated they had the right to extend it for any length of time the U.S. government deemed necessary. If I went against it and tried to quit, my ass would've been tossed into Leavenworth, and my family would *still* think I was dead."

Juliet sat quiet for several minutes before asking, "You said you no longer worked for the CIA. So, when did you..."

"Get out?" he finished for her. "Two years ago."

"Two years..."

Mike could practically see her wheels turning. "The investigation into your dad and his operation was my last job."

She let out a loud breath. "Of course. It all makes perfect sense, now."

"It does?"

"Sure it does. You got what you wanted. Dad and Ivan went to prison, I was forced into protective custody, and Mikhail..." Her eyes widened. "Did he know?"

"Not at first," Mike answered honestly. "I told him later."

Juliet's lips curled into one of the saddest smiles he'd ever seen. "You're the reason he testified."

"Yes."

"So, you're the reason he's dead."

Mike swallowed a huge-ass ball of guilt and told her the truth. "If you want to blame me for Mikhail's suicide, you can. But the truth is your dad did put that wheel in motion before you or I were ever even born."

Her hand went to her mouth and tears fell down her cheeks. "You destroyed my family."

"Alexandar did that. He and Ivan both. Not me."

"My god." She pushed herself to her feet and walked woodenly into the living room. "Why were you at my house that night? Was it because my father was granted a new trial?"

"No."

Juliet spun on her heels to face him. "That's it, isn't it? Your friends in the CIA heard Dad had been released...that he was granted a new trial and might go free."

"No."

"They sent you back in, didn't they? That's why you were there the night Schreiber broke in. You didn't just happen to show up at the right time. You were watching me. Waiting until I needed you so you could swoop back into my life to do what? Use me against my father?"

"Goddamnit, *no!*" Mike stormed across the room to her. "I tried to stay away. God help me, I tried. Not because I wanted to, but because I knew you deserved better than someone like me. Someone who's lived half his life not knowing who he was going to be from one day to the next."

His chest heaved and he forced himself to draw in a handful of slow, deep breaths. Juliet just stood there staring at him as if she were trying to figure out what was real and what was total bullshit.

Join the fucking club.

"I told so many lies back then to so many people back then, the truth damn near became unrecognizable. But then I met you, and the truth became so clear. Yes, I used your brother to gain access to your father. Yes, at first, I thought maybe I could do the same with you, but then I got to know you. I fell in love with you. After that, everything I did...everything I'd become was about protecting you."

Mike blinked against the burning in his eyes. He didn't even notice the tear that had escaped one of them until he felt it hit his cheek and roll off of his chin.

With an angry swipe of his hand, he wiped his face dry and continued on. Continued fighting for the one and only woman to ever make him see past the bullshit.

She made me want a future.

"The day that FBI prick Fuller came and took you away, I fought with everything I had to get him to see you weren't like the rest of them. That you weren't like your father or Ivan, and you knew nothing about your dad's sex trafficking business. But he wouldn't listen. Neither would Ben. No one, not the CIA or the FBI, would fucking *listen!*"

Mike ran a frustrated hand through his hair, grabbing a clump and squeezing. A million little pinpricks of pain spread throughout his scalp before he finally let go.

"I wanted to tell you," he whispered to her. "I can't even count the number of times I almost did."

"Maybe it was all those times we made love?" Her lips formed a sneer. "No, wait. We didn't make love. We had sex. Hot, sweaty sex that meant absolutely nothing."

"You're wrong." Mike took a step toward her. "I may have lied to you about my name and my job, but I never, *ever* lied about my feelings for you."

"I wish I could believe that." Silver streaks fell down her cheeks, but she wiped them dry.

"Baby, you can." He closed the distance between them, thankful when she didn't back away. "Don't you see? You know everything, now. And we still don't know who's after you, which means you still need my protection. We can use this time together to start over."

"I want to start over!" she yelled, her voice echoing off of the cabin's thick walls. Then she huffed a breath, almost as if she were laughing at herself. "No, that's not true. Part of me does want that, which is so fucking stupid. I mean, I find out you've been lying to me this entire time, and yet part of me still wants to be with you."

It wasn't a declaration of love and forgiveness, but her words still made Mike want to do a fist pump in the air. If there was even a tiny part that still wanted him—and she'd just confessed that there was—that meant he had a chance.

"It's not stupid, Juliet. You love me. And I love you."

Her brows turned inward as if she were fighting against herself. Fighting was good. That meant she was considering it, which was a hell of a lot more than he expected. Or deserved.

That's right, sweetheart. You know I'm right. You just have to let yourself see it.

"I know this won't happen overnight." Mike pressed forward. "But I swear to you, if you'll just stay here with me, I'll prove to you that what I feel for you is real. I'll spend the rest of my life proving to you that what we have together is *real*."

She walked over to the cabin's large, picture window and looked out at the surrounding landscape. With the softest of voices, she asked him, "Do you remember our walk down to the river?"

He remembered it had been a nice, pretty day. But he'd focused more on the beautiful woman sitting next to him than the scenery.

"Of course, I do."

"We were sitting there, looking out over the river. It was so quiet and peaceful, and I thought, this is it. *This* is what I want our life to be like."

Turning around slowly, she faced him once more. The sad, almost tortured expression on her face gutting him raw.

"We can still have it, Jules." He risked moving in a little closer. "Baby, we can have any kind of life you want. Just name it, and it's yours."

"I want that life." She blinked setting free yet another set of twin tears. "I want it with *you*, but..."

Mike covered the remaining distance between them. Slowly, giving her plenty of time to move away if she wanted, he brought his hands toward her, cupping her face. "I want that with you, too, baby."

"But how?" Her voice cracked. "I don't even know what to call you anymore."

"Call me whatever you want, baby." Mike stared deep into her ocean blue eyes. "As long as you call me yours."

Her breath stuttered inside her chest. "I don't know what to believe anymore."

"Believe in this, Juliet." He pressed his lips to hers in a barely-there kiss. "Believe in us."

She opened her mouth to respond, but an alarm sounded on his phone, cutting off whatever she was about to say.

Shit. "It's the gate. Damn it, I have to check it." Mike brushed his thumb across her soft skin. "I have to keep you safe."

Pulling his phone from his pocket, he opened the security app Ben had him download in order to access the property's cameras and, if necessary, open the gate remotely.

The image appeared, and Mike damn near broke the phone when he saw the face of the man waiting at the gate.

Sonofabitch. "You've got to be kidding me."

"What's wrong?"

"Fucking Fuller."

Juliet frowned. "The FBI agent?

"That's the one."

"What the hell is he doing here? Did Ben send him?"

"I don't know." Mike tapped his screen to allow the gate to open. "But we're about to find out."

He wanted to continue their conversation, but with Fuller headed their way, they were forced to table it. For now.

While they waited for the prick to make it down and around the road to the cabin, Mike shot off two fast and furious texts to Ben. One to let him know what a dick move leaving that folder with Jules had been and another asking why the fuck the asshole FBI agent was here and how he even knew where to find them.

The CIA agent responded almost immediately, answering Mike's second question with a vague as shit explanation. The asshole completely ignored the first one.

Juliet hugged herself nervously while they waited for Fuller to arrive. By the time the dickhead pulled up, the entire cabin had become filled with thick, nervous energy.

Mike had the front door open before the man had fully exited his car. "What the fuck do you want?"

"Nice to see you, too, Bradshaw." The man glanced at Juliet from over Mike's shoulder. "Oh, shit. Sorry. You still going by Reynolds, these days?"

"It's Bradshaw, and she knows everything so cut the crap and tell me why you're here."

"Why do you think?" Fuller made his way up the porch steps. "I'm here, for her."

"Fuck off." Mike backed up and started to close the door, but Fuller's foot got in the way.

"I have a court order to take her in."

Mike pulled the door open again. "The hell you do."

"It's right here. Judge's signature is barely dry." He waived a folded bunch of papers in Mike's face. "Just like old times, isn't it?

Snatching the papers from the man's hand, Mike unfolded them and scanned the documents. His heart sank.

"This is bullshit, and you know it." He smacked the order against Fuller's chest. "This didn't work before. It's not going to work this time."

"That's where you're wrong." Fuller took the papers and shoved them into his jacket pocket. "You see, last time Juliet's dipshit of a brother was here to run interference for her. But since Mikhail decided to put a bullet through his brain, your sweet little piece, here, has no choice but to testify against her father."

"You son of a bitch!" Mike filled his fists with the front of the fucker's pressed shirt. Pushing him back across the porch, he didn't stop until he had Fuller's back shoved up against one of the structure's wooden pillars. "You don't ever disrespect her like that again, you hear me?"

"My, my, Michael." Fuller smiled. "I do believe you're truly smitten with the little bitch."

Mike's fist was flying before even realized he'd moved.

"Don't!" Juliet was behind him, her hands pulling him away from the arrogant asshole. "He's not worth it."

"That's assaulting a federal agent, Bradshaw." Fuller smoothed the wrinkles on his shirt. "I could arrest you for that."

"Do it." Mike dared him. "You won't."

"You're right. I won't. I will, however, be taking her in." Fuller reached around him and grabbed Juliet's wrist.

"Get your hands off her!" He pushed the prick back.

Fuller swung his fist around, the punch catching Mike square in the jaw. The unexpected move caught him off guard, and a dizzying pain exploded on the left side of his head.

He went down. Hard.

Fuck that hurt!

"No!" Juliet was there, crouching down and trying to help him. She looked up at Fuller and yelled, "You asshole!"

"I may be an asshole, but at least my daddy didn't sell underage pussy to the highest bidder. Let's go." Grabbing hold of Juliet's arm, Fuller used his free hand to pull his weapon and point it at Mike. "Try to stop me again"—Fuller warned—"and I'll shoot your ass."

Seeing double, Mike licked a drop of blood from the corner of his busted lip and said, "Someone is trying to kill her, Thomas. If you take her, you're putting her in danger."

"She'll be with me, dumbass. There isn't a safer place for her to be." The FBI douchebag yanked Juliet to her feet and pulled her down the steps.

"Jules!" Still dazed, Mike finally managed to push himself into a standing position. A dizzying wave hit, but he kept his footing and moved toward the edge of the porch. "Goddamn it, Fuller. Don't do this. You're gonna get her killed!"

"Sorry, Bradshaw. I'm just following orders."

Mike's gaze shot to Juliet's. A look of resolve filled her defeated eyes as she stared back at him.

"This isn't right, and you know it!" he yelled at the other man.

"I don't give a fuck if it's right or not." Fuller opened the passenger door and shoved Juliet into the car. "Like I said, I'm just following orders."

Heading down the stairs, Mike started for Juliet's side of the car but froze when Fuller raised his weapon once more.

"I wouldn't do that if I were you," Fuller warned.

Goddamn it!

Mike's gut told him the man would gladly pull the trigger. His gut was also screaming at him that the whole situation was way the fuck off.

"I'll get you out." Mike spoke to Juliet through the windshield as Fuller holstered his weapon before climbing behind the wheel and shutting the door. "I swear to God, I will."

He was rewarded with a ghost of a smile and a tip of her head.

She doesn't believe you.

Fuller put the car in reverse and spun it around."

"I love you!" Mike shouted, praying she could still hear him.

He wasn't sure, but he could've sworn he saw her mouth the words back to him just before Fuller turned the car completely around. It sped down the driveway and out of sight, carrying with it the most precious thing in his world.

Mike stumbled back up the stairs and into the house. His jaw hurt like a bitch, and his head throbbed, but it was nothing compared to the pain he felt in his chest.

He glanced down at the folder Ben had dropped by earlier. Opening it, he began skimming through the paperwork.

"What the fuck?"

Inside the folder were copies from the first case he'd ever worked for the man. Flipping through the papers, Mike searched for something, anything that could possibly relate to Volkov. He found nothing.

He brought the wrong fucking file.

"Unfuckingbelievable."

Ben stops by while he's in the middle of the fucking woods to bring him a worthless file. Then he hands the file to Juliet, knowing it had his real name right there, on the top fucking piece of paper.

Rubbing his chin, he couldn't help but chuckle at the irony of it all. With a shake of his head, Mike pulled his phone from his pocket to call the asshole but stopped.

A strong, nagging feeling formed deep inside his gut. He went back through the entire chain of events, from the time Ben left the file to now.

It wasn't right. Something wasn't. Fucking. Right.

Mike called Jake, surprised when he answered before it barely had time to ring.

"I was getting ready to call you."

Something about his brother-in-law's tone heightened his already off-the-charts level of anxiety. "What's wrong?"

"I just got off the phone with Alexandar Volkov."

"*What?*" Mike's stomach dropped. "Why the fuck would he call you? Better question, how the hell does he even know who you are?"

"He didn't say. But he also knows who you are. Apparently, he has since before we showed up at his place."

As far as what-the-fuck moments went, this was a pretty substantial one. Mike began to pace.

"Why didn't he say anything?" Or shoot their asses the second they stepped foot on his property?

"I asked him the same question. Said he knew how you felt about his daughter, and that you'd do whatever it took to keep her safe. Figured your protection was better than anything he could provide, so...he went along with it."

"Jesus Christ."

And the hits just keep on coming.

"Exactly. After we left, Volkov started digging. Looking for anyone with a motive to hurt him or Juliet."

When Jake didn't say more, Mike damn near shouted, "And?"

"Mike...Volkov thinks his son Ivan is behind the attacks on Juliet."

"Ivan? Why the hell would he want to hurt his sister?"

"According to Alexandar, the same lawyer who got him a new trial thinks he can do the same for Ivan. For reasons he didn't bother sharing, Alexandar was willing to take his chances, even if it meant Juliet were to testify against him this go around. But Ivan—"

"Wouldn't," Mike finished for his friend. "Motherfucker."

"It gets worse."

Worse than Juliet's own brother taking out a hit on her?

"While he was in prison, Alexander became best buds with one of the guards," Jake continued on. "He's been his eyes and ears ever since he got out, and apparently he's picked up on a lot of shit. Mostly about how, once he's released, Ivan plans to take over the family business."

"But if Alexandar's released for good, too, then how can he...ah, fuck." The horrifying realization hit Mike square in the chest. "Ivan's planning to take out his father, isn't he?"

"Alexandar believes so, yes. First he has to get rid of the one person he believes will stand in the way of his release."

Juliet.

"You get a name?"

Since Ivan is still behind bars, he'd have to have someone on the outside doing his dirty work. Someone smart enough and ruthless enough to orchestrate the attempts on Juliet's life.

"I did, and...you're not going to like it."

At first Mike didn't understand what Jake was saying. Then, as if the stars of hell had suddenly aligned, he understood.

"It's Lopez, isn't it?"

"I'm sorry, man."

He let loose with a long string of curse words. Storming around the cabin, Mike wanted to hit something. No, he wanted to hit Lopez.

"I'm going to kill him," he growled.

"Mike."

"No, Jake. I'm serious. I'm going to rip his fucking heart out of his chest and shove it down his goddamn throat."

"Mike..."

He paced some more. "He was here, you know?"

"Lopez? When?"

"About an hour ago. Asshole stopped by to give me some bullshit file. I was outside cutting wood, so he gave it to Jules, and..." He stopped walking and frowned. "Wait. He was here in the cabin alone with her, Jake. He had the perfect opportunity to take her out, then. Why didn't he?"

"Lopez is smart, Mike. Think about it. He knew you were close by. He does something to make Jules scream or whatever, you come running. You see him, his game is over."

"So why even stop by in the first place?"

"My guess? He wanted to check out the situation. See if your guard was down, maybe?"

"The file he gave her had my real name in it, Jake. Juliet knows the truth."

"How much of the truth?"

"All of it." The betrayal in her eyes would probably haunt him forever.

"Wait a minute. Lopez drops by, hands Jules a folder he knew would blow your cover, and then leaves." It was a comment, not a question.

"I know." Mike shook his head. "It doesn't make any sense."

"Actually, it does."

He frowned. "How?"

"The fucker knows if he can put a wedge between you two, it makes her vulnerable. More susceptible to someone else's influence. Someone like, say, a government agent."

"Lopez left, remember? He didn't even lay a finger on her."

Thank fuck.

"And he won't."

"I'm not following you."

"Think about it, Mike." Jake tried to make him understand. "Lopez hasn't been doing this shit on his own. He wasn't the one who broke into Juliet's house in Houston. He didn't pull a drive-by on your place or blow it all to hell. A guy like that...that's not his style."

His mind finally began to catch up. "He'd need someone else to do it."

"Someone with enough authority to make luring her away from you seem legit."

Someone with authority...a government agent...

"Fuller."

"Who?"

"Ah, God." Mike doubled over and tried to breathe. His physical reaction to the fact that he'd just watched the woman he loved drive away with a killer was enough to damn near bring him to his knees.

The room began to spin. The throbbing returned. His chest heaved with the effort it took to draw in a full breath, and it was all he could do not to empty the contents of his stomach all over the floor.

"Mike?" Jake's voice sounded muffled. "Goddamn it, Mike. Talk to me!"

Juliet needs you. Pull yourself together, Bradshaw. She needs you.

Legs quivering, he stood and put the phone back to his ear. "He's got her, Jake."

"Who?"

"Thomas Fucking Fuller. He's FBI."

"How the hell did he—"

"He was here, too. About ten minutes ago. Had a court order to take Juliet into protective custody so she could testify against her father. I looked it over, but...shit. I was pissed and...damn it, it could've been fake, for all I know."

Motherfucker!

With an animalistic growl, Mike swiped his hand across the kitchen table, the move sending the file and all of its contents flying through the air.

"Keep it together, man," Jake urged. "We're going to figure this out. We'll get her back."

"You're over two hours away, Jake." He went into the kitchen. Opening one of the drawers, he grabbed the keys to the truck Ben had left for them to use. "I'm all she's got."

Storming across the room to the front door, Mike pulled his coat from the peg and got the shotgun and pistol from the small gun safe positioned in the far corner.

Ben had left those for him, too. For protection from any predators they may encounter. The arrogant son of a bitch left him armed because he didn't think he'd figure this shit out.

You were wrong, asshole.

Slamming the cabin door behind him, Mike jogged down the porch steps and made his way to the truck. Placing the two weapons onto the passenger seat, he fired up the truck and put it into gear.

"What are you going to do?" Jake asked.

Mike pushed the pedal to the floor and gravel spewed as he spun the truck around. "I'm going hunting."

Chapter 14

Juliet stared out her window feeling...hell, she didn't know *what* she felt, anymore.

Lost. Betrayed. Heartbroken.

Okay, so maybe she *did* know. She felt all those things and more. She just didn't know what to do about it.

Not much you can do.

She glanced at the man driving the car. FBI Special Agent Thomas Fuller. Tall and broad, he looked more like a linebacker than a government agent.

And if he thought she was going to do anything for him after the way he'd treated her and Mike, he was even dumber than he looked.

"I won't help you," she stated clearly. "So, if you want my father back in prison, you're going to have to find another way to do it."

"I didn't take you so you could testify, sweetheart."

Wait. What? "Then why..."

Keeping his left hand on the wheel, Agent Fuller reached into his jacket and pulled out his gun. The barrel was pointed directly at her ribs.

"Get the picture now, or do I need to spell it out for you?"

Juliet's veins turned cold, fear leaving her momentarily frozen. "Why?"

"Why does anyone do anything?"

She was struck with a strange case of déjà vu, and it didn't take but a few seconds to figure out the cause.

Why does anyone do anything? Money, sweetheart. And your father has a helluva lot to spare.

Aaron Schreiber, the man who'd broken into her townhouse, had said those words to her. Right before he died.

"You sent Schreiber to kill me, didn't you?"

"I did."

There was one mystery solved, but she still needed to know who this asshole worked for. If he was getting paid to do this, that meant there was someone else involved. Someone bigger than Fuller who was willing to pay a shit ton of money to make her disappear forever.

"Is it my father?"

"Is what your father?"

Talk about spelling shit out. "Is he the one who's paying you to do this?"

"Right." Fuller snorted. "Daddy's little princess? Please. Your father wouldn't hurt a fucking hair on your clueless head."

Mike's gut had been right. And yeah, it also occurred to her that somewhere along the way, she'd begun to think of him as *Mike* instead of Jay.

Her chest physically hurt from the aching in her heart. From his lies, yes. But also because she knew he'd blame himself for her death.

I love you.

Hearing him shout that at her from outside the car had crushed her. Seeing the pain and regret and fear pouring off of him as Fuller drove them away? That had damn near broken her.

I love you, too.

She'd mouthed those words back to him. Had he seen them? Did he know that, despite his deception, at her core she still loved him?

Holy shit. I still love him.

The shocking revelation left Juliet blinking. It was crazy. Certifiable, even. Hell, she had no idea if they could still make things work after the stunt he pulled.

One thing she did know, was that if she gave up and let this bastard kill her without at least putting up a fight, she'd never know what might have been.

Screw that.

Right then and there, Juliet decided she would *not* give up. That she would fight this bastard with everything she had. But she needed a plan.

Her only chance at survival was to get out of this car and away from Fuller. Her mind raced and swirled with possible scenarios and outcomes, and soon, a plan started to form.

Distract him. Keep him talking.

"If my father didn't hire you, then who did?"

"Does it matter? You'll be dead soon, either way. And I'll be on a plane to the Marshall Islands." He glanced over at her and grinned. "It's a stretch of islands between Hawaii and Indonesia. Beautiful weather...sandy beaches. But the best part? No extradition treaty with the U.S." He chuckled to himself. "See? You shouldn't think of your death as a meaningless waste. Think of it as my retirement plan. I'll make it quick and painless for you. The money I get for taking you out pays for a life filled with suntans and babes in bikinis. It's a win-win, really."

Jesus, this guy was a piece of work. "What?"

"Are you deaf?" He glowered over at her. "I just told you the whole plan. I kill you, I retire in the Marshall Isla—"

"No, I mean what makes you think I care?"

Yeah, the comment was snarky and immature, but damn it felt good. It was also part of the plan she'd just derived...

Get him worked up, take the gun, and voila. Problem solved.

A muscle in his large jaw bulged. "Fuck you."

"Thanks." Juliet smiled. "But you're not really my type."

"Keep it up, and I'll shoot your smart mouth right now."

"See, I don't think you will." At least she hoped and prayed he wouldn't. "You shoot me now, my blood and brains will be all over this car. A car that has your fingerprints all over it." She tipped her head toward the steering wheel. "Not to mention all the nooks and crannies blood splatter can slip into."

Guess all those times spent eavesdropping on her dad and his friends when she was little were good for something, after all.

"That shit won't matter." Fuller shook his head. "Not where I'm going."

He sounded sure of himself, but the wavering gun said otherwise.

"That's the thing," Juliet continued on with her little speech. "As we were driving away, Mike mouthed something to me."

Fuller smirked. "He told you he loved you. Fucking pussy."

"I'm talking about after that."

"Fine, I'll play along. Not like there's anything better to do...until it comes time to kill you, that is. So tell me, what did your little boyfriend have to say?"

"He mouthed the words 'it's him' and pointed to you."

"I didn't see him do that."

Because he hadn't. It just popped into her head, and she thought it sounded like a good thing to say. She had no idea what she was doing, other than trying to distract him long enough to get the gun.

"You were focused on the road. That's why you didn't see him, but I'm telling you the truth. He must've realized it at the same time we were leaving. Either way, he knows you're not the upstanding Federal agent you claim to be."

"What do you know?" Fuller grinned. "The tattooed fucker finally got something right."

"He did," Juliet agreed. "Something else you should know is Mike's boss owns a private security company. Now, I haven't had a chance to learn all the ins and outs of it, yet, but I've been on his private jet, and let me tell you...it was *nice*."

"What the hell does that have to do with anything?"

Despite the fact that she was shaking like a leaf inside, she held it together and gave the man a casual shrug. "A jet like that costs big bucks, right? Big bucks means there's a slew of money coming in. You do the math, Fuller. A security company with that much income has to have some pretty good connections."

He slid her a sideways glance. "So?"

"*So*, more than likely, Mike's already called his boss to tell him about you. If I were his boss, and I'm sure the guy's much smarter than I am, I'd report your ass to every airport in the country. Use those contacts to get you on a no-fly list. Which means, you kill me and dump my body in a ditch somewhere, you're still not getting to those islands you've been dreaming about."

"Good thing Mike's boss isn't the only one with a private jet."

Shit. "Let me guess. Your boss has one, too?"

"Technically it's my boss's boss. Pretty sure you've been on that one a time or two, as well."

She had? Juliet thought for a moment before it clicked. "You said my father didn't hire you."

Her dad used to have a small jet...before the government seized it and the rest of his assets he hadn't had time to hide. Apparently, no one bothered sharing that with Fuller.

Because he's a pawn. They're using him to do the dirty work, then they're going to kill him, too.

"He didn't." Fuller looked over at her. "Ben Lopez hired me. And Ivan hired him."

Ivan?

No amount of effort could hide her reaction to that particular surprise. It wasn't as if she and Ivan had ever been close. Definitely not as close as she and Mikhail had been. Still...

"My brother has a CIA agent and an FBI agent trying to kill me?" Juliet turned her stunned expression onto Fuller. "Why, to protect my father?"

"Fuck no." The unattractive sound escaped the back of the man's throat. "Your father's the next one on my list."

"He wants us *both* dead? Why would Ivan—"

"Jesus, you really are dense." Fuller huffed out a breath. "Why do you think? Ivan wants to be in control. He's taking over, and your father's in the way. It's already in motion, he just needs the both of you gone to seal the deal."

Juliet's brain felt like it was going to explode, and her emotions were running on serious overload. Between Mike's big reveal, and then thinking she was going back into protective custody, only to learn that Fuller had been hired to kill her by her own brother...

If I survive this, I'm going to need a serious vacation. And counseling. Lots and lots of counseling.

With a mental shake of her head, she got herself back on track. "If Ivan's wanting to take over, then I guess getting Dad out of the way makes sense. But why me? I made it clear a long time ago that I wanted nothing to do with any of it."

"Fuck me, I guess I do need to spell it out for you." Fuller sighed. "It all starts with you, sweetheart. Apparently, the high-dollar attorney Daddy hired is the same one representing Ivan. He got your dad a new trial based on a technicality, and since the cases were intertwined, he thinks Ivan will be granted one, too. But if you're around to testify..."

The final piece of the twisted Volkov family puzzle fell into place. "They'll *both* be sent back to prison for good."

"Now you're gettin' it." He rolled his eyes. "If Ivan gets sent down the river again, he's screwed. You disappear, your old man kicks the bucket, and Ivan goes free. He's sittin' pretty, and so, am I."

While Fuller started rambling on again about the grand plans he had for the rest of his miserable existence, Juliet's mind wandered to the insanity of the whole situation.

She'd always known she was born into a messed-up family, but this had to be some kind of record. The blood running through her veins was tainted in ways most people could never even fathom.

Her thoughts turned to Mike, and she began to question *his* sanity. Why would a guy like him want to give her the time of day, much less try to have an actual relationship with her?

Maybe he was just as crazy as the rest of them. Maybe he was the one in need of counseling. Maybe he...

Loves you.

The voice in her head was right. Mike may have lied about a lot of things, but that wasn't one of them. She could see it in his eyes when they'd made love. In the way he'd gone at Fuller in her honor.

For months, the man had lived every day surrounded by the darkness her family had bestowed upon this world, but despite it all, he still loved her. And right or wrong, she loved him, too.

Which meant she couldn't let him live the rest of his life blaming himself for whatever this asshole had planned for her. She needed to act. Now.

Juliet glanced down at the gun, which was pointing down at her leg rather than her ribs. Getting shot there would still hurt like a bitch, and there was always a chance the bullet could hit her femoral artery, but it was less risky than one to the heart.

Checking to make sure his eyes were still on the road, Juliet held her breath and said a quick prayer. Then, before she could talk herself out of it, she went for the gun.

"What the hell?" The car swerved when he tried pulling the weapon out of her hands. "Are you fucking crazy?"

Not crazy. Determined.

Using all of her strength, she pushed the barrel away from her. If she could twist it in his hands enough, she could—

The gun went off, filling the car with a deafening boom. Juliet's ears began to ring, but she could still hear Fuller's roaring scream as the car made a sudden jerk to the left.

She was thrown against the howling man's side, and the gun fell to the floorboard, sliding beneath Fuller's seat.

"You shot me, you fucking bitch!" His hand flew in her direction.

A sharp, thundering pain exploded in her left cheek and eye. Juliet cried out but blinked against the white dots filling her vision. She couldn't pass out, now. If she did, she was a dead woman.

With his right leg bleeding like a stuck pig, Fuller reached beneath his seat in search of the gun. Knowing she couldn't let him get to it, Juliet did the only thing she could think of.

She grabbed the wheel and jerked it hard in her direction.

Fuller's large body flung to the right, and he tried to regain control of the vehicle. It was too late.

Hoping her seatbelt and airbags would be enough, she held onto the *oh, shit* handle and waited. The car ran off the road and down into a ditch, taking air before its tires found the ground again.

Juliet and Fuller bounced around like rag dolls, and at one point, she felt her head smack against the passenger window. She barely had time to register the pain before a large tree came into view, stopping the car on impact and sending her into a dark and peaceful oblivion.

****

"I don't see them, Jake. I don't *fucking* see them."

Mike sped down the two-lane highway in search of Fuller's car. Of all the shit he'd done, all the fucked-up messes his undercover time had forced him into...he'd never experience true terror until now.

"Keep looking," Jake spoke calmly. "You said they didn't get that big of a head start, right?"

"They didn't, but shit. What if I'm going in the wrong direction?" *What if I can't find her in time?*

"You're going the right way."

"How the hell can you possibly know that?" Mike pushed the gas pedal as far down as it could go.

"Because I know you, and I trust your gut. You need to do the same."

"I'm trying but...fuck. I can't lose her, man. I *can't*." But that was exactly what was going to happen if he didn't catch up to them soon.

Mike's stomach revolted at the thought. He'd always known he would die for Juliet. What he didn't know was how he was supposed to live without her.

"Listen to me, Mike. I know it's hard, but you've got to pull your head out of your ass and stop thinking that negative shit."

The road in front of him blurred with a well of unshed tears. "I can't help it."

"Yes, you can. And before you ask, I know you can because I've had to do it." Jake sighed. "Thinking I was going to lose Liv was the hardest fucking thing I've ever gone through. But I got through it, and so did she."

His sister's smiling face flashed behind his eyes. "I know, man. I know, but this is—"

"Different?" Jake cut him off. "The only difference between then and now are the players. I'm telling you, Mike...the best piece of advice I got then is the same thing I'm telling you, now. Treat this like an op. Stay focused, know your goal, and do what it takes to reach it."

Mike knew his brother-in-law was right, but this was Jules. She wasn't just some nameless hostage on an op. She was his life. She was...

"My everything."

"I know she is, man. Which is why you've got to get your head in the game."

Shit. He hadn't meant to say that out loud, but Jake was right. Goddamn it, he was *right*. Juliet was on her own with Fuller, and if he didn't lock down his emotions right the fuck now, he might lose her forever.

Blinking away the remainder of his tears, Mike sat up straight and cleared his throat. "Okay."

"Okay?"

"Yeah, man. I'm good."

He could practically hear Jake's smile when he said, "Welcome back."

As serious as the situation was, Mike found himself grinning. "Smart ass."

"Better than being a dumbass."

Through the phone, Mike heard someone else talking in the background. "That D?"

"Yeah. He just got here. I'll put him on speaker."

"Hey, man," Derek greeted him. "I'm tracking your phone, and I've got you pulled up on the GPS."

"Good, because I'm looking up ahead, and all I see are trees, trees, and more fucking trees."

"I'm sure you can feel it, but you're on a steady incline. That road goes up into the mountain you're currently on, but it levels out before long and then starts to go back down."

"Anything else that might be good to know?"

"Just that you'll want to stay on the paved road. There's a trail not far from where you are now, but all it leads to is a pretty steep drop-off."

A horrifying image of Fuller taking Juliet there tried working its way into Mike's mind, but he shoved that shit away and remained focused.

"Copy that."

Mike drove a couple of miles farther, and just when he was starting to give up hope, something up ahead caught his eye.

"I see something." He squinted his eyes for better focus. "It's hard to tell from here, but it almost looks like...ah, fuck."

"What?" Jake and Derek spoke in unison.

"It's Fuller's car."

"Wait, you found them?" Jake asked.

"Maybe."

Derek spoke up next. "What exactly do you see, Mike?"

"I see Fuller's car...or what's left of it. Looks like the asshole lost control. He ran it into a goddamn tree."

Several low curses hit Mike's ear, but all he could focus on, all he could *think* about, was that Juliet had been in that car, too.

As he got closer, he could make out the skid marks on the pavement and gouges in the grass. "I'm pulling onto the shoulder where the car went off."

"Watch your back, dude," Derek warned. "There are a fuck ton of trees around there. Plenty of places for that douchecanoe, Fuller, to hide.

"D's right," Jake offered up his two cents. "You don't know what you're going to walk up on so stay alert."

Stopping the car, Mike grabbed the pistol from the passenger seat and jumped out. "I don't know whether to be touched or insulted."

This wasn't his first rodeo, and both men damn well knew it.

"Just stay focused, asshole," Jake grumbled. "Remember the goal."

"Trust me, it's the only thing I'm thinking about." Mike raised the gun and started walking toward the wreckage. "I'm putting my phone into my pocket, so I can use both my hands. I'll keep it on, though, just in case."

Jake surprised him when he said, "Ryker's got some guys headed your way, since we can't be there ourselves to give you backup."

Jason Ryker was a Homeland Security agent and R.I.S.C.'s handler when they took on jobs for the government agency.

"Ryker?" Mike jumped the ditch and ran up the opposite incline. "I thought you told him to go fuck himself after the shit he pulled with Bravo Team a while back."

"I did. This is one of the many things he's doing to make up for it."

Bravo Team was the other R.I.S.C. security team. From what Mike had heard, some shit went down with that team's leader, and Ryker had played a part in letting it happen.

"I'll keep an eye out for them, too."

Mike started to put his phone into his pocket when he heard Jake's voice again.

"Hey, Mike?"

"Yeah?"

"Your sister will never forgive either of us if you get your ass killed."

He smiled. "Don't worry. The only one dying today is Fuller. Maybe Lopez if I can track his ass down, too."

"Copy that."

With the phone away, Mike used both hands to keep the gun steady as he approached the mangled car. He watched for any signs of movement, but all he saw was the steam dissipating into the air above the car's crumbled hood.

The closer he got, the more conflicted he felt. From what he could tell, it didn't look like Juliet or Fuller were in the vehicle. That meant they hadn't been killed when it rammed into the tree.

Thank you, God.

It also meant, they both were out there, somewhere. Jules was quite possibly injured.

Forcing himself to stay focused, he kept his gun trained as he made his way around the back to the driver's side. Both the driver's and passenger's seats were empty, and Mike's first reaction was relief. Then he saw the blood.

Fuck.

There was a lot of it. Enough to make him believe whoever it belonged to had been hurt in a pretty significant way.

Horrified at the thought of it being Juliet's, it took him a few seconds to realize the blood was in the driver's seat. Not the passenger's. Which meant it belonged to Fuller.

Keeping a close eye on his surroundings, he grabbed his phone and updated the others. "They're not in the car, but Fuller's seat is covered in blood, so I'm pretty sure he's hurt."

"Any sign of him or Jules?" Derek asked anxiously.

"Negative. The passenger door is hanging open, and there's some blood on the window. Not a lot, though. She probably hit her head when the car lost control."

The thought of her being hurt in any way killed him, but at least Fuller seemed to have gotten the worst of it. Mike looked down by his feet and noticed a trail of blood leading from the car into the trees.

He smiled. "I can track them."

"Ryker's men are about ten minutes out, Mike," Jake informed him. "Wait for them before you go into those woods."

Something cold and wet hit Mike's nose prompting him to look up. He blinked as several large snowflakes peppered his face.

"Juliet doesn't have ten minutes, Jake." He headed into the forest. "She's out there, somewhere, running for her life from that prick, and it just started to fucking snow. I gotta go."

Unable to afford the distraction, Mike decided to end the call. Shoving the phone back into his pocket, he kept his eyes on the blood and did exactly what he'd set out to do.

He started hunting.

Chapter 15

Juliet ran. Her head and chest hurt, there was blood running down the right side of her face, and if she were a guy, her balls would be frozen by now. But she kept running.

Waking up in the car with Fuller next to her had been terrifying. Thankfully, the crash had knocked him out, too.

Would've been better if the bastard was dead.

It was the first thing she'd checked when coming to, and Juliet had actually cried a little when she saw his bulky chest rising and falling. Normally, she'd never wish anyone dead. But this situation was as far from normal as she'd ever been.

Knowing he'd kill her the second he woke up, she hadn't wasted any time unbuckling and getting herself out of the car. Her initial thought was to run to the road, but then she remembered how desolate the area was.

Plus, if Fuller did come after her and she was out in the open, he'd have a clear shot. Being an FBI agent, Juliet knew if he were given the chance, the man wouldn't miss.

So, she'd run into the trees.

Juliet had been running for what seemed like forever, but she didn't dare stop. She wanted to, especially after the numerous times she tripped and fallen. But she didn't.

Her speed had started to taper off, however, and though she had some cover from the evergreen's branches, the snow that snuck through only made things worse.

What started as tiny, sporadic flakes had almost instantly changed to huge, fat ones that were accumulating quickly. She thought of the coat and gloves still hanging on the peg back in the cabin and kicked herself with every step for having taken it off when she had.

Her teeth chattered, and though she couldn't see them, Juliet suspected her lips had turned a nice shade of bluish-purple. If she didn't get herself out of these trees and someplace with people who could help her, she may not have to worry about dying by Fuller's gun.

That was another thing she was kicking herself for. Not grabbing the gun before she ran. But in her defense, she'd just woken up from having blacked out and her thought processes were slightly impaired. Also, she'd been terrified that Fuller would wake up to find her body over his while she searched for the damn thing.

"You can't run forever!"

Juliet's footing stuttered and she tripped again. That time when she fell, she stayed down and listened closely.

Was that voice real, or did I imagine it?

"Come on, Juliet. It's too cold to be doing this shit. Just come back here, and we'll go find help together."

Oh, God! It's really him!

Ignoring the pounding in her head and the pain in her chest, Juliet jumped to her feet and took off, again. Several yards later, she caught site of a long stretch of white opening through the trees.

It was hard to tell if it was a road or what, but she decided to go for it, all the same. As she got closer to it, she realized it was too narrow to be an actual road. A trail maybe?

Trails lead to things. Maybe this one would lead her to people...and a phone she could use to call Mike.

Her heart ached worse than her head, but she gritted her teeth and forced all of that away. Letting herself travel down that path would most certainly deter her from what needed to be done.

Small, white clouds escaped Juliet's mouth with each breath as she broke through to the trail. She knew her boot prints would lead Fuller straight to her but avoiding them in the ever-accumulating snow was an impossible feat.

She'd just have to push herself faster. Put as much distance between them as possible. Best case scenario, his injury would slow him down enough for her to escape.

Worst case, he'd catch up to her and kill her. But hey, at least she'd die knowing she tried.

A tiny, hysterical laugh bubbled up and was set free. Juliet instantly rolled her lips inward to cut off the sound. If he heard her, he may be more motivated to keep coming.

Her body trembled, and her goosebumps had goosebumps. Her boots felt heavier and heavier with each step, but damn it, she couldn't give up. She couldn't...

There!

Juliet spotted a large clearing up ahead. The ground was covered, and the densely falling snow made it almost impossible to see anything beyond it, but it had to mean something. The edge of someone's property, maybe?

Her renewed hope brought with it a sudden burst of energy. Juliet pushed herself harder. Faster. And before she knew it, she was at the trees' edge and running through the clearing.

Big, fat snowflakes kept landing on her lashes, but she blinked them away. A chilly breeze blew past, instantly freezing several strands of her long, dampening hair, but she brushed them off her face and kept going.

You've got this, baby. Don't give up.

It was as if Mike was by her side, cheering her on.

She smiled, picturing his handsome face and those heart-thundering eyes. Soon her imagination and wishful thinking began to take over, and before she knew it, she'd reached the end of the clearing...and the edge of a very sharp, very deep cliff.

Juliet cried out, her outstretched arms mimicking a helicopter's blades as they swirled about at her sides to keep her from falling. The toes of her boots hung over the land's edge and clumps of snow tumbled down into the wintery abyss.

Looking down, her heart thumped against her ribs when she got her first good look at what was almost her grave.

Steep, uneven walls seemed to go on forever, their surface littered with sharp edges and a few trees that had managed to find their way through the cracks.

A narrow river divided the deadly cavern. Its edges lined with piles of rocks that meant instant death for anyone unlucky enough to fall.

With her breath frozen in her lungs—almost literally—Juliet carefully slid herself back away from the ledge. First her left foot, then her right. She didn't stop until there was a solid yard between her and the drop-off.

Exhaling slowly, Juliet's chin quivered as she released a long, slow breath. Her entire body shook, the sweater and jeans she'd put on this morning useless against the frigid air. But she was still alive, so she had to keep going.

She turned away from the cliff to assess her surrounding and decide which direction to travel in next. But the man limping toward her—and the gun in his hand—prevented her from going anywhere.

"You're a f-fighter." Fuller trudged closer, the slowly trickling blood leaving drops of pink in his snowy wake. "Gotta...g-give you th-that."

Tears froze at the corners of Juliet's eyes. "Why don't you j-just leave m-me here?" Her numb lips and chattering teeth made it difficult to talk. "I'll d-disappear. Use a different n-name. N-no one will ever know I'm s-still alive."

This was her last chance. A hail Mary. If she could talk him into letting her go, then maybe she could find her way back to Mike before she developed full-blown hypothermia.

Mike had lived for ten years under different names. If anyone could help her vanish, it was him.

"N-nice try...p-princess. No b-body...n-no paycheck."

Shit. "I'll pay you d-double. M-Mike can get you out of th-the c-country."

"M-man of my word, p-princess." The gleam in his soulless eyes doused whatever hope she'd felt a few minutes before.

He's enjoying this.

Having had enough of his sick games, Juliet shouted at him. "You b-bastard!" Her voice echoed through the winter air. "Your w-word doesn't m-mean sh-shit!"

"Doesn't...m-matter." He grimaced as he hobbled even closer. "Any final p-prayers you've got...you'd b-better say them n-now."

Panic set in and Juliet wanted to howl to the universe at the unfairness of it all. She wasn't ready to die. In many ways, she'd barely even begun to live.

They say your life flashes before your eyes right before you die. But the only image Juliet's saw in her mind's eye was the man who'd stolen her heart.

Mike was her soulmate. Her other half. And despite their unconventional beginning, Juliet knew he was the man she was meant to find.

I'm so sorry, Mike.

Fuller straightened his stance, preparing to shoot. Juliet closed her eyes, ready to accept her fate. Holding on to the last remnants of dignity she had, she stood there, waiting for her life to come to an end...and then she heard it.

She heard *him.*

"Drop the weapon, Fuller!"

Juliet's eyes flew open, and she couldn't believe what she saw.

"Mike!"

He was still several yards away, and the snow was still falling in sheets, but there was no mistaking that face. Running toward them, he appeared to be carrying a gun of his own. Its barrel was pointed directly at Fuller.

Fuller.

The man was turning around, too. His gun moved with him, away from her, and toward...

"No!" Juliet didn't think. She just reacted.

Reaching out, she grabbed Fuller's arm and pulled it back. The sound of the bullet firing through the barrel echoed all around them, but thankfully she'd prevented it from going anywhere near Mike.

"Jules!"

Fuller pushed against her, doing his best to force her to let him go. Her feet slid in the snow, and she felt herself moving backward, but she held on with everything she had.

"F-fucking b-bitch!"

The strong man swung his elbow toward her face, but Juliet saw it coming and managed to move just in time for him to miss.

"Let her go!"

Mike was getting closer, now. Close enough he could shoot Fuller.

Realizing this, as well, Fuller let out a loud roar and shoved Juliet again. No matter how hard she tried, she couldn't hold on.

Juliet fell backward, the snow doing very little to break her fall. With an *oomph*, she landed hard on her back, her head inches away from the edge of the cliff. She was pushing herself back up to her feet just as another shot rang out.

No!

Her heart flew into her throat, but when she raised her head, she discovered it wasn't Mike who'd been shot. It was Fuller.

The killer-for-hire dropped his gun and stumbled backward. Fresh blood dripped from his right hand, the warm drops melting the snow the second they hit.

Finally managing to become upright once again, she started to move out of the way for fear the injured man would accidentally knock her over the deadly wall. In an unexpected move, Fuller turned his focus back on her.

With a hatred and fury unlike any she'd ever seen, he raised his un-injured arm and reached for her. Screaming, Juliet tried to move to the side, but her foot slipped, and she went down on one knee.

Mike fired his weapon again, the second shot hitting his target with perfection. Blood oozed from the new hole in Fuller's chest. Right where his heart would be, if the bastard actually had one.

The large man took several steps backward. Juliet could tell he was about to go down...and she was right in his path.

"Juliet!" Mike shouted her name. He was running toward her and waving his arms, signaling for her to move.

Scrambling to get away, the snow and her frozen form made standing more difficult than it should've been, but she finally managed to get herself upright.

She took a step forward—toward Mike—right as Fuller's limp body collapsed against her. She lost her balance, and though she tried desperately to find purchase, the snow was simply too slick.

Mike's terror-stricken eyes grew as wide as saucers, and his screams of denial echoed through the mountains. But it was too late.

Juliet felt herself falling, and this time, there was no snowy ground below to stop her.

****

"No!"

Mike's stomach dropped, his lungs seizing with fear as he watched Juliet disappear over the edge of the cliff.

Running as fast as his legs would take him, he slipped and nearly went down twice as he raced to save the woman he loved.

Please, God. Please, let her be okay!

The snow swirled in front of his face as it was carried by the freezing wind. The blizzard-like conditions made it almost impossible to see more than a few feet in front of him, which was why Mike had hesitated to shoot Fuller sooner than he had.

With Jules standing so close to him, he hadn't wanted to risk hitting her. He hadn't wanted to chance something happening and her going over the fucking edge.

Oh, God.

The idea that he may have just watched the woman that he loved die was enough to end him.

"Juliet!" His throat burned as he screamed for her. "Baby, talk to me!"

Refusing to believe she was gone, Mike dropped to his knees at the spot where he'd seen her go over. Praying for a miracle, he held his breath and leaned out over the edge.

"Mike!" Juliet's voice reached him from below.

Tears of overwhelming relief flooded his eyes when he saw her. She was alive. His sweet, loving, incredible woman was *alive*. And hanging onto a broken branch.

Fuck! "Hang on, baby! I'll get you up!"

"Hurry! M-my toes caught the edge of a r-rock, but its slick and I keep s-slipping."

Jesus. Even from here, he could tell she was on the verge of becoming hypothermic. How she'd managed to grab the branch when she fell, let alone keep herself from tumbling to her death, was beyond him.

She could still fall.

Springing into action, Mike laid flat onto his belly. Ignoring the breathtaking cold, he scooted to the edge as far as he could without losing too much of the supportive ground below him.

Dangling his right arm over the edge, he dug the fingers of his other hand as deep into the frozen ground as he could.

"Here!" He reached for her. "Grab my wrist and hold on tight."

"Won't I p-pull you over?"

"No, baby. I've got this."

She hesitated. "I'm scared. What if I c-can't hold on to y-you?"

"It's okay." He looked into her terrified eyes and vowed, "I'll hold on to you."

Nodding, she'd just started to let go when one of her toes slipped from the jutting rock she'd been balanced on.

She screamed and Mike shouted her name, nearly going over the edge himself in an effort to save her. Miraculously, Juliet kept her grip on the branch and was able to regain what little footing she'd had before.

Mike closed his eyes and said a silent prayer of thanks before opening them back up and trying again.

"Come on, Jules. You can do this."

"I'm g-going to f-fall."

"No, you're not. Now, grab hold of my wrist and let me pull you up."

She lifted one hand off the branch, keeping herself in position with the other. With slow, careful movements, she wrapped her ice-cold fingers around his thick wrist and held on as tightly as she was able.

"Good girl." He blew out a breath. "Now the other one."

He could tell she was trying to talk herself into it, which was great except the colder she got, the worse her grip was going to become.

You need to get her ass up here. Fucking now!

In all the time they'd spent together, Mike had never said a cross word to her before. But desperate times called for doing whatever the fuck needed to be done. So...

"Goddamn it, Juliet," he yelled. "Let go of the fucking branch and grab my fucking arm!"

She let go of the branch. She grabbed his arm. Mike started to pull her up.

"Don't...let...go," he shouted through clenched teeth.

The muscles in his right arm burned from the strain. Tendons stretched to their maximum potential, and his shoulder felt as if it were precariously close to popping out of place.

He didn't even consider stopping.

Almost there. Just a little more...

Mike let out a loud roar, the animalistic sound filling the air around him as he ignored the pain and gave one final pull. It wasn't until Juliet was over the edge and in his arms that he realized it had come from him.

"Oh, thank God." He held on tightly. "I thought I lost you."

"Th-thought you had...t-too."

She trembled and shook so violently against his body, he felt it deep inside his ribs. As much as he hated letting her go, they needed to get off the ground and somewhere warm as soon as possible.

He stood and helped her do the same. "Come on. Let's get you to a hospital."

"D-don't need a h-hospital." She pulled him to a stop and looked up at him. "Only n-need...y-you."

Does she mean that, or is it the cold talking?

A shiver raced down his spine, making him think it was probably the latter.

Mike squeezed her hand and started to walk. "You're freezing. We need to—"

She pulled on his hand again. This time, the crazy woman grabbed his face, rose to her tiptoes, and pressed her ice-cold lips to his. "L-love you, M-Mike."

She called me Mike.

His heart swelled to the point he thought it would burst from his chest. The woman had fallen off a cliff, and damn near died and she was frozen from head to toe, yet she'd stopped to tell him she loved him, and she'd called him *Mike*.

Ignoring how cold his ass was or how weak his right arm felt after the workout he'd put it through, Mike bent down and scooped her into his arms.

"I love you, too, baby." He kissed her again. "God, I love you so much."

Juliet opened her mouth to say something else when they heard multiple male voices in the distance. They turned and saw three bulky men walking down the trail toward them. All three were carrying guns.

Mike started to reach for his when one of them held up a hand. "You Bradshaw?"

"Who's asking?"

"I'm Reid. This is Beckett and that's Stone." The men continued advancing. "We do some work for Jason Ryker. He said you could use some backup?"

Relief flooded him because, fuck. He was cold as shit and did not feel like shooting their asses, too.

With Juliet held snuggly in his arms, Mike made his way to the newcomers. "Thanks, but...you're a little late."

"Sorry, man," Reid apologized. "Fucking snow slowed us down."

"She hurt?" The one named Stone asked. He removed his heavy coat and laid it over Juliet as best he could.

"There a hospital nearby?"

"T-told y-you—"

"You're getting checked out." Mike gave her a no-nonsense look.

Rather than argue further, she smiled and laid her head against his chest. Even though her voice was small and muffled, he still heard her soft, "Okay."

Epilogue

"I still can't believe she gave your ass a second chance."

With a smile, Mike selected a few poker chips from the stack in front of him and tossed them in the center of the table. He looked over at Grant. The former SEAL and Alpha Team's demolitions expert seemed even grumpier than usual.

"Truth?" Mike picked up the card Trevor had dealt him. "I can't either."

The men who were still in took a second to look at their cards. A minute later, Mike was pulling the pile of chips in his direction.

"Don't pay any attention to Hill." Derek grinned. "He's just pissed because he hasn't won a hand all night."

Grant scowled at the other man. "I'm pissed because you fuckers keep cheating."

The men around the table all began laughing and talking at once. Glancing at the group of women sitting across the room, Mike grabbed his bottle of beer and stood.

"Deal me out this next round. I need a refill."

"A refill." Jake looked down at the half-full bottle in Mike's hand and gave him a knowing grin. "I know what that's code for."

Mike smacked him on the shoulder as he walked past. "Like you're any better?"

"How do you think I know the code?"

Cringing, Mike turned and hollered at the man from over his shoulder. "That's my sister you're talking about, dickhead."

"What's your sister?"

Stopping in his tracks, Mike spun his head around and found Olivia standing directly in front of him. "Your husband still hasn't learned to not talk about your sex life in front of me."

His sister grinned. "Well, I *am* an adult, and as you pointed out, he *is* my husband. So, yeah...we do have sex."

"Lots of it!" Jake yelled loud enough for everyone to hear.

Groaning, Mike flipped his friend the bird. "Doesn't mean I want to hear about it."

"Speaking of hearing about things..." His sister grabbed his arm, bringing his attention back to her. "Has Jules seen it, yet?"

"Seen what?" Juliet stepped up beside Olivia.

"It was *supposed* to be a surprise." With a playful glare thrown in his sister's direction, Mike slid his focus to the woman of his dreams. "I'll show you later."

"Oh, come on. Show her now." Olivia pretended to pout. "Please?"

Juliet mimicked her new friend's expression. "Yeah, please?"

He fought against the smile threatening to break loose. "I think I liked it better when she didn't know you were my sister."

"Which is the perfect segue into the surprise!" Olivia's face lit up.

Losing the fight, Mike's mouth curved into the same, goofy smile he'd been walking around with for the last few weeks.

"Okay, fine."

He went over to the kitchen bar and set his bottle down. Juliet looked up at him, her gorgeous face filled with curiosity. Standing behind her, Olivia looked like a kid at Christmas while she waited for his big reveal.

"It's really not that big of a deal. Just something I got today that I thought you might like."

"He got it while you and Mac and I were shopping earlier," Olivia piped in.

Mike shot the meddling woman a look. "Do you want me to show it to her or not."

Acting like the little sister he knew and loved, Olivia stuck her tongue out at him and then winked at Juliet.

With a shake of his head, Mike chuckled as he reached down and grabbed the hem of his shirt. Lifting the left side, he showed her the addition to his tattoo collection.

He wanted it to be as close to his heart as he could get it, but he also wanted it to stand out. To stand alone. Since he already had ink that covered the top portion of his chest, he decided to put this one near his side, just below his left peck.

Juliet's sharp intake of air was audible when she saw the word 'Trust' permanently embedded into his skin. She didn't say a single word. Juliet just stood there, staring.

He had no idea whether or not that meant she loved it...or hated it.

"I got it for you," he blurted like a nervous schoolboy. "Well...for us."

She continued staring but still said nothing.

Shit. Fuck. Shit.

Mike's heart kicked his ribs as he tried to make her understand. "I wanted you to know that, from this point on, you can trust me. *Really* trust me."

Juliet stepped toward him slowly, her eyes never leaving the new ink. She lifted her hand and began tracing the scrolling letters with the tip of her index finger.

His muscles contracted, the skin there was still a little tender. But he'd be damned if he ever told this woman to stop touching him.

"It's okay if you don't like it. I can always—"

She cut him off with an unexpected kiss. "I love it," she whispered against his lips.

"Yeah?"

Juliet nodded. "Yeah."

"Good." Dropping his shirt, Mike wrapped his arms around her waist and pulled her body flush with his. "Because you can trust me, baby. Always."

He was rewarded with another quick kiss. "I know I can."

"I love you, Jules."

"I love you, too, Michael J. Bradshaw."

With a huge grin, Olivia stepped up beside them. "See? I told you she'd love it."

Juliet smiled back at his sister. "I can't believe you didn't slip and say something about it when we were out shopping."

"Um...excuse me, but my brother isn't the only one in the family who can keep a secret."

"Yeah, well." Mike pulled Juliet to his side. "From now on, the only secrets I'm keeping will pertain to Christmas and birthdays."

"Ahem." Jake joined them. "And anything R.I.S.C. related that I deem classified or confidential."

The four laughed, but then Olivia and Jake shared a strange look before she said, "Do you have it with you?"

"You want to give it to them now?"

His sister nodded. "Why not?"

"Guess there's no time like the present." Jake nudged his wife and smirked. "See what I did, there? No time like the *present*...because this is a present, and—"

"Yeah, Jake." An unimpressed Olivia patted her husband's shoulder. "We get it."

Make the guy a dad, and he becomes king of the dad jokes.

With a roll of his eyes, Mike looked at the couple and said, "Will one of you please tell me what the hell you're talking about?"

"This." Jake pulled an envelope from his back pocket and handed it to Mike.

Confused, Mike used his free hand to grab it while asking, "What's this?"

"Just open it."

Releasing Jules, he ripped open the envelope and pulled out the folded papers. He skimmed the documents, and it took him a minute to realize what he was even looking at. When he did, his jaw dropped open.

"You're giving us part of your land?"

"Not just any land." Olivia smiled. "The forty acres on the back half. Where the river cuts through it."

Mike knew exactly which piece of land she was referring to. Minus the mountains, it had a view that was pretty damn close to the spot on Lopez's land that Juliet had loved so much.

"I don't know what to say."

"Nothing to say, brother." Jake squeezed one of Mike's shoulders. "You seemed ready to finally put down some roots." In a not-so-subtle move, his gaze slid from Mike's, to Juliet's, and back to Mike's. "We figured what better place for you to do it than close to family?"

"There's plenty of space for a house and whatever else you two might need. Plus, you'll be able to see your adorable baby niece anytime you want," Olivia added as a bonus.

Mike thought of the little girl currently sleeping in the bedroom down the hall. Then he thought of another little girl. The one he'd imagined the last time he was here.

The little girl with the black hair and striking blue eyes...just like Juliet's.

Though it wasn't that long ago, it seemed like a lifetime had passed since then. It was amazing how much could change in just a few weeks' time.

He'd reconnected with Juliet, and then he damn near lost her. Fuller was dead and Lopez had been arrested and had plead guilty to being an accessory in Schreiber's death and conspiracy to commit murder.

The Federal prosecutor was able to keep Mikhail's original testimony as admissible, and Juliet's dad went back to prison where he belonged...without her having to testify against him. Three days after Alexandar Volkov returned to prison, Ivan Volkov was found dead in the shower by one of the prison guards.

As so often occurred with such things, no one heard anything, and no was saw anything. As far as Mike and Juliet were concerned, justice had been served.

The best part of the whole damn mess was that, in the end, Juliet still loved him. The *real* him. They'd been living together in a rented apartment in the city ever since, and with the help of the other R.I.S.C. women, she was already making contacts to start up her own interior design business.

For the first time in what felt like forever, Mike could honestly say that life was good.

He thought about the woman by his side and the deed in his hand, and a sudden burning sensation spread over his eyes. Mike blinked his unshed tears away, knowing if he started crying in front of the guys, he'd probably never live it down.

"Wow." Juliet sounded amazed. "What an incredible gesture."

"I missed out on a lot of time with my brother," Olivia told her. "I'd love to have him close by. We want you *both* to be close by."

Their time together—both before everything happened with Fuller and after—had been such a whirlwind, they hadn't really talked about the future all that much. They'd just relished in the fact that they were together. But now that Jake and Liv had brought it up...

"What do ya say?" Mike turned to Juliet. "Wanna build a house together and live out here in the wide, open spaces?"

"Come on, Jules," Olivia pleaded with her. "You and I could have girls' nights whenever we wanted. Oh! You could even bring Lydia over so Lillian could play with her."

"Lydia did seem to love it here." Juliet smiled.

"But?" Mike held his breath and waited.

"Not really a but, per se. More like a condition."

"Name it, it's yours."

Juliet raised a brow. "Will this house in the country come with a nursery?"

Mike's heart stopped beating. "You're pregnant?"

"No." She chuckled. "I was just thinking...you know...someday."

Pulling her to him once more, Mike leaned down and pressed his lips to hers. With his eyes staring down into the future he'd thought was an impossible dream, he said, "I think someday is a damn good place to start."

****

"A guilty verdict has been handed down today in the Federal case against former CIA agent, Benjamin Lopez, and several other arrests have been made in connection with the crimes for which Mr. Lopez has been convicted. We'll have more on this story as it unfolds."

"Hey, Riley! You're up."

Riley York's long, dark ponytail flung over her shoulder as she turned away from the T.V. above the bar and walked over to where her partner was standing.

Her heart stuttered inside her chest every time she looked at him, which was dangerous given their department's policy regarding romantic relationships between partners. But with his light brown hair and blue eyes, the man was walking, talking sin in a suit.

Taking the wooden pool cue from Eric's hand, she studied the ever-changing table in front of her before deciding which move she should make next.

"I see Lopez is going away." He nodded toward the T.V. she'd just been watching.

"Yep. Bastard got what he deserved. So did Thomas Fuller." She spotted her next target. "Five ball, side pocket."

Moving like a pro, Riley bent over the table's edge and lined the cue up. Positioning it between the fingers on her left hand, she bit her bottom lip, took aim, and made the shot. The five-ball rolled across the green felt, falling into the side pocket with ease.

"Nice shot."

She shot him a grin. "Thanks. That's another drink you owe me."

"What does that make, now. Five?"

"Six." She sauntered up to him and raised a brow. "You're losing on purpose."

One corner of Eric's delicious mouth rose into a guilty grin. "Now, why would I go and do something like that?"

"Same reason you keep bringing me to this hole-in-the-wall bar on the opposite side of the city from our precinct." Riley handed him the pool cue.

"Why, Detective York." Eric pulled the cue—and Riley—to his chest. "Are you accusing me of trying to take advantage of you?"

"Of course not." She rose onto her toes and rubbed the tip of her nose to his. "It's me who's planning on doing the taking."

"Oh, yeah?" He nibbled her bottom lip. "Well, in that case, we should—"

"Hey, turn that up!" One of the patrons sitting at the bar yelled loud enough to break the spell. "And hurry up. My old ears can't hear for shit."

"Yeah, yeah. Keep your panties on, Walt. I'm gettin' it."

Riley and Eric both looked up at the T.V. as a bright red Breaking News banner flashed across the bottom of the screen.

"We interrupt this program to bring you breaking news. A body of a young woman has been found near the banks of Trinity River. The police are still working on identifying the victim of what they are calling an obvious homicide."

"Shit." The beer in Riley's stomach churned as she listened to the anchorwoman continue on with the story.

"While we have not been told whether or not this case is related to Jennifer Hanway's or Marie Paul's deaths, our source did say that the DPD has found several similarities in the three women's murders. You might remember, both Hanway's and Paul's nude bodies were also found near the Trinity River, the coroner's report showing that both women had been sexually assaulted before they were strangled. We'll bring you more on this story as additional information becomes available."

"Jesus," Eric muttered with a shaking head.

Riley worked to keep her breathing steady. "That's three, Eric."

"Yeah, but the Trinity River covers a lot of real estate, Riles. We have no idea where the bodies were found in relation to each other, how this newest woman died...nothing. Besides, it's homicide's case, and those guys are solid. They'll figure it out."

Eric was right. There was no known evidence linking these newest deaths together. Just because they reminded her of an old case meant nothing. Besides, the killer in that case was dead, which meant it couldn't be him.

Shaking off the uneasy feeling the new murders had conjured up, Riley looked up at her partner and smiled. "You're right. It's not our case, and we have tomorrow off."

"Yes, we do. Now..." Setting the pool cue to the side, Eric wrapped an arm around her waist and pulled her back in. "Where were we."

"I think you were about to invite me back to your place."

You know"—Eric leaned in for a kiss—"I think you're right."

With a soft chuckle, Riley closed her eyes and allowed herself a moment of guilty pleasure. Not that she was embarrassed or ashamed to be seen with Eric. Quite the contrary. Any woman in her right mind would be thrilled to be involved with a man like him.

Eric West was smart, sexy, and one of the best damned detectives she'd ever worked with. He was the whole package and then some. But he was also her partner at the Dallas Police Department's Special Crimes Unit.

While their Captain—who'd known Eric for years—had a sort of soft spot when it came to Eric, he had no such history with Riley. The newest detective in their division.

Not to mention, she was also female. In her experience—especially at her old department—that meant she had to work harder and be better than any of the men she worked with.

So far, she hadn't experienced anything like at her old job. But she didn't want to press her luck, either. Which was why, when she felt herself growing more *personal* feelings for Eric, she'd played it cool.

It worked, too. But then he started showing interest in *her*.

At first, it was just playful teasing between the two of them. She'd make a smartass comment and he'd come back with a smartass quip. They'd banter about everything under the sun, but at the end of the day, they were an amazing team that got the job done.

The dynamics worked for them for a while...until it didn't.

The closer they became, the harder Riley fell for him. The harder she fell, the harder she tried to fight it, until her suddenly cool demeanor toward him started causing problems on the job.

Determined to resolve their issues, Eric had shown up at her apartment one night after work. They talked. They argued. And then they'd stripped each other's clothes off.

After that night, there was no going back. Not for her, and as far as she could tell, not for him. But with their jobs on the line, they still had to be careful. So they stole a kiss, here. A wink or a smile, there.

And they came to this run-down shack to play pool, drink, and then spend the night devouring each other. Riley knew they couldn't keep this up forever, but for now...for them...it worked.

Pulling away, Eric licked his lips and pulled his phone out to call a cab back to his apartment. Within minutes they were walking out of the bar together and she'd forced all thoughts of death and murders completely out of her mind.

The next morning—after another amazing night with Eric—Riley treated herself to some Starbucks drive-thru on the way back to her apartment.

Feeling deliciously sore in all the right places, she unlocked her mailbox and grabbed the previous day's mail. She was sifting through the handful of junk mail when the building superintendent walked up. "Hey, Riley." The kind, balding man smiled. "This wouldn't fit, so the guy who delivered it left it with me."

He handed her a small, brown box with no return address. "Any idea who it's from?"

"No clue. He didn't say, and I didn't ask."

That's strange. "Okay, Frank. Thank you."

"No problem." He gave her a half-wave as he turned and walked away. "Have a good one."

In her apartment, Riley set the box down onto her dining room table next to the pile of mail and hung her purse on one of the chairs. Sipping her coffee, she studied it with an expert eye.

Upon closer inspection, she found no ticking sound or traces of any sort of powdery substance. It wasn't heavy in the least, and when she shook it, it didn't rattle.

In fact, the box felt sort of...empty.

The detective in her wanted to take the package down to the station and have the forensic guys check it out, first.

"You're being ridiculous," she told herself, and then she went into the kitchen and grabbed a knife from the set next to her stove.

Returning to the table, Riley set her coffee down. She sliced through the brown packaging tape and put the knife to the side.

Pulling the top flaps of the box apart, she looked inside and frowned. Folded up in the middle of the box was a single piece of folded paper. Assuming it was some sort of advertising gimmick, Riley grabbed the paper and unfolded it.

Her breath froze in her lungs when she read the printed words...

Miss me?

Dropping the paper, she stumbled into one of the chairs as she reached for her purse and pulled out her phone.

Hands shaking, she hit the first saved number on her favorites list and waited. Eric answered on the second ring.

"Miss me, already?" he answered in his goofy, teasing voice.

His choice of words sent a shiver down her spine. "Can you come to my apartment?"

"Are you okay?" His voice had turned low and serious. "What's wrong?"

She swallowed hard. "I just need you to get over here. Now."

"I'm on my way." A shuffling sound traveled through the phone and Riley knew he was getting out of bed. "Are you safe?"

She looked down at the note again, the words sending a familiar shockwave of terror through her system. One she vowed to never feel again.

"Goddamnit, Riley, talk to me!" Eric's worried voice broke through her fear. "Are. You. Safe?"

She gave him the most honest answer she could give. "I don't know."

****

Want to read Riley and Eric's story?

Savage Risk (R.I.S.C. Book 8) is Available for Pre-Order Now![1]

Savage Risk Blurb:

HER SAVAGE NEED FOR JUSTICE MAY END UP COSTING HER EVERYTHING

When the criminal who has taunted Riley York for years suddenly reemerges in her new city, she vows to take him down for good. With her partner by her side, Riley will risk everything for one final chance to see justice served.

Until now, Eric West has kept his burgeoning feelings for his partner close to the vest and their personal relationship casual. But all that changes when things turn personal and Riley becomes a killer's next target. With his heart and life on the line, Eric will stop at nothing to keep the woman he loves safe.

With help from R.I.S.C.'s Alpha Team, these two detectives will face their most dangerous opponent yet, one hellbent on destroying Riley's happiness—and her life—forever.

---

1. https://www.amazon.com/Savage-Risk-R-I-S-C-Book-8-ebook/dp/B08NH1H3TJ/ref=sr_1_1?dchild=1&keywords=savage+risk&qid=1607052098&sr=8-1

Want to read more from Ms. Blakely's R.I.S.C. Series?

See how it all started with Jake and the rest of Alpha Team by checking out the other books in this series:

Book 1: Taking a Risk, Part One[1] (Jake & Olivia's HFN)
Book 2: Taking a Risk, Part Two[2] (Jake & Olivia's HEA)
Book 3: Beautiful Risk[3] (Trevor & Lexi)
Book 4: Intentional Risk[4] (Derek & Charlotte "Charlie")
Book 5: Unpredictable Risk[5] (Grant & Brynnon)
Book 6: Ultimate Risk[6] (Coop & Mac)
Book 7: Targeted Risk[7] (Mike & Jules)
Book 8: Savage Risk[8] (Eric & Riley)
Book 9: Undeniable Risk[9] (Ryker & Sophie)

---

1. https://www.amazon.com/TAKING-RISK-PART-R-I-S-C-Book-ebook/dp/B07KV1WN2M/ref=sr_1_1?ie=UTF8&qid=1545935537&sr=8-1&keywords=taking+a+risk+part+one

2. http://bit.ly/TakingaRiskPartTwoAmzn

3. http://bit.ly/Beautiful_Risk

4. https://www.amazon.com/s?k=intentional+risk&ref=nb_sb_noss

5. https://www.amazon.com/Unpredictable-Risk-R-I-S-C-Book-5-ebook/dp/B08121Q22T/ref=sr_1_1?keywords=unpredictable+risk&qid=1583071266&sr=8-1

6. https://www.amazon.com/Ultimate-Risk-R-I-S-C-Book-6-ebook/dp/B083BGX9VR/ref=pd_sim_351_1/136-7699527-9116030?_encoding=UTF8&pd_rd_i=B083BGX9VR&pd_rd_r=c6105876-607b-4f69-bd90-b969a3900acb&pd_rd_w=GnGzP&pd_rd_wg=VpL69&pf_rd_p=65e3eab0-d81f-4a76-93ff-f0b7b1d6cd3d&pf_rd_r=CT47DHN02D3Q25JEF1DZ&psc=1&refRID=CT47DHN02D3Q25JEF1DZ

7. https://www.amazon.com/dp/B088SND1VZ/ref=sr_1_2?dchild=1&keywords=targeted+risk&qid=1589837961&sr=8-2

8. https://bit.ly/SavageRiskAmazon

9. https://bit.ly/UndeniableRisk_Amazon

Book 10: His Greatest Risk[10] (R.I.S.C. Series Finale)

---

10. https://bit.ly/HisGreatestRisk_Amazon

Check out R.I.S.C.'s Bravo Team!

Click below to read Ms. Blakely's R.I.S.C. spin-off series in Susan Stoker's
Special Forces: Operation Alpha World:
Book 1: Rescuing Gracelynn[1] (Nate & Gracie)
Book 2: Rescuing Katherine[2] (Matt & Katherine)
Book 3: Rescuing Gabriella[3] (Zade & Gabby)
Book 4: Rescuing Ellena [4] (Gabe & Elle)
Book 5: Rescuing Jenna ~ Releasing January 2020

---

1. https://amzn.to/2KOap0o

2. https://www.amazon.com/Rescuing-Katherine-Special-Forces-Operation-ebook/dp/
   B085GH6HQQ/ref=sr_1_1?dchild=1&keywords=rescuing+kather-
   ine&qid=1589836951&sr=8-1

3. https://www.amazon.com/gp/product/
   B08C45WWYQ?pf_rd_r=TQEKRB704P6TQ6GK3YCB&pf_rd_p=edaba0ee-
   c2fe-4124-9f5d-b31d6b1bfbee

4. https://www.amazon.com/dp/B08M3RDDZ2/ref=sr_1_2?dchild=1&keywords=rescuing+el-
   lena&qid=1603895874&sr=8-2

Taking a Risk, Part One Blurb

(Book 1 in Ms. Blakely's R.I.S.C. Series)

"From the first book Taking a Risk to the 6th Ultimate Risk I have truly found a new favorite author. Susan Stoker, Kris Michaels & Riley Edwards are three of my very favorite authors, but Anna Blakely is now among those. I have loved those first 6 books. Please try these books you can't go wrong. You'll know I'm right when you start reading the first book. Trust me it won't take you long."

- Amazon reviewer

HE LOST HER ONCE. HE'LL DIE BEFORE LOSING HER AGAIN.

Growing up, she was his best friend's little sister. For years, he's kept his distance. Now, it may be too late.

Former Delta Force Operator Jake McQueen can handle anything...except losing the only woman he's ever loved. Driven by an intense need for revenge, Jake and the other members of R.I.S.C travel deep into the jungle to find those responsible for killing Olivia, and to make them pay for shattering his entire world. What Jake doesn't expect to find is his very own miracle.

SHE'S FIGHTING AGAINST HERSELF.

After narrowly escaping a fate worse than death, Olivia Bradshaw gets a second chance at life...and love. Still devastated by the violence she's been forced to endure, Olivia struggles to overcome her paralyzing guilt and shame. But if she doesn't find a way to forgive herself, she'll never be able to accept the love Jake is finally offering.

THEY'RE BEING HUNTED.

When they're forced to separate from Jake's team, these two must make their way through the sweltering jungle. Because someone wants Jake dead...and to have Olivia for themselves.

Will these two make it out alive, or will the future they've only just begun to explore be lost at the hands of their enemies?

*Author's note: TAKING A RISK, PART ONE is a full-length novel, and is the ONLY R.I.S.C. Book with a cliffhanger ending. This is Jake and Olivia's Happy-For-Now, while TAKING A RISK, PART TWO is their Happily-Ever-After. Jake and Olivia's story was simply so complex and intertwined, theirs took two full-length books to complete. ALL R.I.S.C. operatives will get their own happily-ever-after...they just have to work for it, first!

Chapter 1 from Taking a Risk Part One by Anna Blakely:

Something was wrong. Very, *very* wrong. The metallic scent of copper filled the air as a red stain appeared on Cody's chest. Olivia's eyes locked with the young male nurse as his gray shirt quickly became saturated with his blood. Yet, she remained frozen. Her own body and mind battling against her efforts to understand.

Moments before, a series of thundering pops had filled the warm, humid air. Time stood still while men continued to yell. Screams echoed all around her, and still, she felt no fear. Olivia felt...nothing.

Her gaze slid back up to Cody's face. His always hilarious—and often inappropriate—jokes had kept their spirits raised in the midst of such devastation. Looking at him now, though, Olivia didn't see his contagious smile. Instead, she found a face twisted with pain. Eyes that were filled with confusion and fear. Then, like a puppet losing its strings, Cody's body went slack, his muscles rendered useless.

She watched numbly as his head slumped forward, and he slid from the log upon which he'd been sitting. Cody landed with a sickening thud in the dry dirt. Olivia was still trying to comprehend what was happening when another terrified scream pierced the air.

Turning slowly, she saw that, much like Cody, the rest of her new friends had begun to fall. Movement to her left caught her attention, and she looked back just in time to see Malani, the young woman who'd lost so much in the storm, drop to the ground by her feet.

Wide eyes stared into Olivia's, their rapidly expanding pupils conveying the fallen woman's desperate plea for help. Seconds later, Malani's head tilted to one side; her beseeching gaze no longer there. Olivia realized that *nothing* was there anymore.

No light. No laughter. No life. If Olivia didn't know any better, she'd almost think that Malani was—

Dead.

The word slammed into her with brute force, bringing Olivia back from wherever her shocked mind had escaped. The scene sped into focus, and she finally, *finally* understood. Her group was under attack, and with an indescribable horror, Olivia realized she was the only one still alive.

Dear God.

Adrenaline surged through her body as her belated fight or flight response kicked into gear. She shot up from her log and spun around in a dizzying attempt to assess her situation.

Several men—at least ten—were quickly approaching. They appeared local and, with one exception, were all dressed in head-to-toe in camouflage, each carrying an automatic rifle at their side.

Olivia's initial thought was to fight but going up against these men would be suicide. She was far too outnumbered, not to mention unarmed.

The well-dressed man headed straight for her. He wore all black, from his dress shirt down to his shiny, black shoes. He would have reminded her of a Wall Street businessman if not for the long, jagged scar running down the right side of his face. The puckered mark, paired with the set of deadly eyes now focused solely on her, sent waves of terror pulsing through her veins.

Instinct told her this was the man in charge, and given the way he was looking at her now, Olivia knew she was as good as dead. Despite her odds, she refused to just stand there, waiting to be slaughtered. She had a snowball's chance in hell of escaping, but she still had to try.

With one final look at Malani and her other fallen comrades, Olivia bolted toward the road leading away from their camp. She thought she heard laughter coming from behind her, but the sound of her own blood rushing through her ears made it impossible to tell.

Leg muscles burned as she forced them to work harder than ever before. Tears fell from her eyes as she thought of her dad and brother. Of the mother she never really knew.

Her entire family was already gone—taken from her far too soon—and Olivia found herself praying that when the bullets hit, she wouldn't have to wait long before seeing them again.

Another image flashed before her eyes. One that nearly brought her to her knees.

Jake.

More tears came as Olivia realized she'd never see her best friend again. Never be on the receiving end of his sexy-as-sin smile or hear his deep-chested laugh.

Even more heartbreaking was the knowledge that she'd never get the chance to say everything she'd always wanted, but, even at thirty-one, she'd been too afraid to. *Why didn't I tell him?*

She should have shared her feelings with him years ago, rejection be damned. At least he would've understood how deeply she cared for him. That just thinking about him could make her smile, even at the worst of times.

A person should know that, right? Everyone needed to know they were loved. *Especially,* someone as good and kind as Jake. And now, it was too late.

Oh, God! A loud sob escaped her throat as she forced her tiring legs to keep moving. She was going to die without ever having the courage to tell Jake she was in love with him. That single thought was more painful than anything these men could ever do to her.

Though she'd never been shot, Olivia knew to the depths of her soul that a bullet piercing her flesh would be nothing compared to the pain searing through her heart at this very moment.

With more thoughts of Jake and a lifetime of regret, she glanced back over her shoulder. The scarred man was right behind her, now. He raised his gun, and Olivia screamed.

She tried to run faster, but it was too late. He was too close, and her body had nothing more to give. She squeezed her eyes shut and pictured the last thing she wanted to take from this world.

Jake's handsome face appeared in her mind's eye. He smiled, the movement deepening the shallow lines bracketing each side of his mouth. His piercing blue eyes sparkled back at her.

I love you.

The words whispered through her mind just before a sudden, sharp pain exploded in the back of her head. And then...nothing.

****

Jake McQueen couldn't think. God Almighty, he couldn't *breathe*. The dizziness and nausea hit him like a freight train as he reached for the remote, desperate to block out the nightmare playing before him. He willed his thumb to press the power button, but his fingers refused to follow the simple order.

"The brief clip you just saw was from the memorial service held yesterday in honor of the eight men and women who were violently murdered in what authorities are still reporting as a drug-related raid. Five weeks ago, the group of American doctors and nurses arrived in Toamasina, Madagascar to offer volunteer medical aid to those in need. As I'm sure most of our viewers already know, Toamasina was one of the many areas devastated by the massive hurricane that hit Madagascar early last month."

Jake shook his head, his denial instant and final because no way, no *fucking* way was this really happening. The media, the so-called authorities...they had to be wrong.

Ah, God, not her. Anyone *but her!*

He continued listening to the TV, searching for something, *anything* that said this was all just some horrible mistake. But the longer he sat there, the more Jake's unwavering wall of denial began to crumble.

Everything he'd just seen and heard pointed to only one truth—Olivia was dead.

Last week, while he and his team had been completing their most recent mission, her entire group had been gunned down. Their bodies burned beyond recognition. A week ago.

Jesus.

Finally regaining some bodily control, Jake raised the shaking remote. He refused to sit and listen to another goddamn word about how she'd been brutally gunned down and then fucking *burned.*

Just then, Olivia's face filled the oversized screen. His thumb froze in place. He couldn't tear his gaze away now if his life depended on it.

Jake knew the picture well. He should, he'd taken it the day Olivia received her nursing degree. She smiled back at him from his TV, her laugh from that long-ago moment forever captured.

A pair of gorgeous, hazel eyes with their mesmerizing swirls of greens and browns bore deeply into his own. They were eyes he'd always sworn he could get lost in. Jake blinked, and her name appeared on the screen in bold letters beneath the picture.

Olivia Bradshaw.

His best friend's little sister. The girl he and her brother, Mike, had spent countless hours of their childhood tormenting...all the while, protecting her with everything they had. She was also the same girl who'd grown before his eyes into the most beautiful, compassionate woman he'd ever known. And the most stubborn.

Olivia had given him so much shit throughout the years, challenging him at every turn. Despite all her sass—or maybe because of it—Jake had never wanted a woman more.

For years, she'd been the star of more fantasies than he could count. The cause of more wet dreams than he'd ever admit. She was also the only woman who'd managed to steal his heart, and last week she'd died without knowing the truth about how he really felt.

A rush of bile hit the base of his throat and Jake barely made it to his kitchen sink before losing the fast-food lunch he'd scarfed down on his way home. A few minutes later, his hands shook so violently that it took three tries to get the damned faucet turned on so he could rinse the rancid taste from his mouth.

After running the garbage disposal, Jake splashed his face with cold water before reaching for the nearest dish towel. In a daze, he wiped the moisture from his skin before tossing the towel aside. His hands became two vice grips, grabbing hold of the sink's edge, his knuckles white from the strain.

Hanging his head between his shoulders, Jake summoning every ounce of his training to force some much-needed air into his lungs. After several controlled breaths, he attempted to calm himself. To accept the unacceptable...Liv was dead.

He thought about the last time he saw her. Regret quickly filled his gut when he realized it'd been nearly two full months. *Too fucking long.*

When his team wasn't away on a job, Jake and Olivia would talk on the phone or hang out whenever they could. Just as friends. No matter how busy they both were, he always made sure he saw her before leaving town again. Except this last time.

His team's most recent job had been the very definition of last-minute. Jake had been home a whopping forty-five minutes and hadn't even had time to unpack his bags from the previous job when he got the call from his handler at Homeland, requesting a hostage location and extraction.

He'd barely had time to shower, let alone see Olivia, before heading out again. So, he left her a voicemail, promising to make it up to her as soon as he got back. Now he'd never get that chance.

Filled with sorrow, Jake squeezed his watering eyes shut. Rather than blocking out the pain as intended, his mind instantly conjured up images from their last day together.

The two had eaten and talked. They'd laughed. More than anything, they'd laughed. *I can still hear her laugh.*

It was always like that with her. They could joke around effortlessly, or just sit in comfortable silence. When it came to Olivia, everything was easy. Especially loving her. So, why the hell hadn't he ever told her? *You know why, asshole.*

Jake had vowed a long time ago never to reveal his true feelings. For several reasons. To start, she was his best friend's little sister. As cliché as it may be, the unwritten rule between guys was very real. You didn't date your buddy's sister...or do anything else with her. Ever.

Sure, her brother had been gone for the better part of ten years now, but when Jake's feelings for Olivia had first begun to change, Mike had still been around. Jake had no doubt that Mike would have kicked his ass from here to Timbuktu if he'd ever known even a *fraction* of the thoughts Jake had entertained about the other guy's sister. Especially the ones involving Olivia naked and in his bed.

By the time she'd lost her brother, there were other, more serious, reasons preventing Jake from taking things further. *Come on, dickhead. Own up to it. It was the fucking lies that kept you from making your move.*

And Jake *had* lied to her. About his job. The way he felt. Then there was *the* lie. The one that had the power to destroy her.

Sometimes, Jake would be with her, and he'd forget. They'd be hanging out, and she'd tell him a funny story about something that had happened in her E.R. He'd be listening to her talk, and the guilt of his betrayal, the secret that years ago he'd sworn to *never* reveal, would momentarily vanish.

Unfortunately, it never lasted. The damn thing was always there, hovering over him like a cloud of poisonous gas, just waiting for the perfect moment to swoop in and destroy the most precious thing in his world.

It didn't matter that every lie he'd ever told Olivia stemmed solely from his need to protect her. Good intentions or not, Jake knew holding on to those secrets meant he'd never get the chance to be with the woman he loved.

It had to be that way. Not only to keep her safe, but also because Olivia deserved the world on a fucking silver platter, and Jake knew he could never give her that.

He did, however, give her as much time as he could between jobs. Since starting R.I.S.C.—the elite private security firm he owned—Jake had actually managed to never leave for an extended op without seeing Olivia first. This last time was the one and only exception.

Not once, though...not one time in all his years had Jake ever considered that he'd get back and *she* would be the one gone.

Ah, Christ. Liv is gone.

His empty stomach convulsed again, and no amount of training could stop it. Minutes later, when the dry heaves finally subsided, Jake's quivering legs managed to take him back to the couch.

He sank down and rewound the broadcast. As much as he dreaded it, Jake needed all the information he could get before determining his next move.

****

Click below to purchase the first part of Jake and Olivia's story:
TAKING A RISK, PART ONE[1]
**ALL R.I.S.C. novels are full-length. Jake and Olivia are the only
couple whose story is split into two books. Taking a Risk, Part
One is their Happy For Now and Taking a Risk, Part Two brings

---

1. https://www.amazon.com/TAKING-RISK-PART-ONE-R-I-S-C/dp/1798654911/

ref=sxts_sxwds-bia-wc-p13n1_0?cv_ct_cx=tak-

ing+a+risk%2C+part+one&dchild=1&keywords=tak-

ing+a+risk%2C+part+one&pd_rd_i=1798654911&pd_rd_r=7f5216bf-2b10-4747-bb28-

98eeb46f2db9&pd_rd_w=Z6FEy&pd_rd_wg=ijc8v&pf_rd_p=d8781cb2-590e-4599-929

9-188f35162ede&pf_rd_r=J02XA8M56KN4G810VD7Q&psc=1&qid=1603654066&sr=

1-1-791c2399-d602-4248-afbb-8a79de2d236f

you their Happily Ever After. All other books in the R.I.S.C. Series are standalones with their own HEA's.

Want to connect with Anna?

Stalk her here...

- Newsletter signup (with FREE book!) BookHip.com/ZLMKFT[1]
- Join Anna's Reader Group: www.facebook.com/groups/blakelysbunch/[2]
- BookBub: https//www.bookbub.com/authors/anna-blakely
- Amazon: amazon.com/author/annablakely[3]
- Author Page: facebook.com/annablakely.author.7[4]
- Instagram: https://instagram.com/annablakely
- Twitter: @ablakelyauthor[5]
- Goodreads: https://www.goodreads.com/author/show/18650841.Anna_Blakely

---

1. http://bookhip.com/

   ZLMKFT?fbclid=IwAR2lZIGJqF5YrRpJSmgph5FGCu9xzhhHoTNFa4yvvQFKPmXMKh2xSoktIpM

2. http://www.facebook.com/groups/blakelysbunch/

3. http://amazon.com/author/annablakely

4. https://www.facebook.com/annablakely.author.7

5. https://l.facebook.com/

   l.php?u=https%3A%2F%2Ftwitter.com%2Fablakelyauthor%3Ffbclid%3DIwAR3eBPASIFhD7

   fc5Uvma8eF1AjPCwmetlIl-

   zEAG669Eg_0amjNhVjuehBA&h=AT19i6MitKZ_vIjaH9n6aV1uqVHausvBKfm12jM2r_D1

   LlIg3g72VbbEiwpffDP3nXHZObcwB4I4xn2YaV_UCl10jr4V6lS4u5wy1bo0ka8ta8x0lEVP5f

   0A5fYaKa3crtTJLg